**COMPROMISED DISCLAIMER:** This is a work of fiction and this statement is included to inform the reader that any celebrity name(s), business name(s), locations, and organizations that are stated in the content of this book are real. However, they are used in a way that is purely fictional.

JAZZY KITY PUBLICATION
PRESENTS

# Compromised

## JERZ TOSTON

Compromised

By: Jerz Toston

Cover Art Created by KREATIVEGRAFIKS.COM

Logo Designs by Andre M. Saunders

Editor: Anelda L. Attaway

Co-editor: Jerz Toston

© 2018 Jerz Toston

ISBN 978-1-7324523-3-6

Library of Congress Control Number: 2018911460

# ACKNOWLEDGMENTS

First, I'd like to thank Allah (SWT) wit out Him this would not be possible.

Next, I would like to tell my kids Kai, Meesh, Jerz, Deivyan, Riya, and Ceer this is all for y'all; never let anyone defer you or tell you that you can't do whatever you want.

All my niggaz from tha 8 Chulo Hammer, Hov, Shafee, and Killer.

My BF's Sissy and Deb.

My sister's Felisha and Nika LOVE Y'ALL.

My Lil' Bro Lbs.

My mother who always push me to be tha best I can be.

My other half, BF, and soulmate Tambra aka Mrs. Toston 2 U thanks for always having my back no matter right or wrong.

Ery body on lock down, Big Marv, John, Dae Dae, Matim, and C-how Imma hold y'all down til y'all touch this side free from tha jails.

To Lil' Bro Cool Shoes Inc., keep doin what you doin for tha youth.

My barber Skills tha nigga that keep a nigga fly weekly.

To ery side of town holding it down.

Gotta say REZ Mom Betty, Moe, Ma5e, H, and my Big Sis Ericka keep watching over me and Imma keep droppin' classics.

Finally, my publisher Jazzy Kitty love ya.

Jus remember wit out loyalty there's no trust & trust is ery thing so always SSSSH hold yours. Y'all got to stop feeding these RATS cheese and embracing them knowing they ain't official Black & White don't lie.

# DEDICATION

This book is dedicated to my niece Jannie Smallwood, u was taken to soon jus kno ur deeply missed & loved.

Rez Baby Girl.

# TABLE OF CONTENTS

# TABLE OF CONTENTS

# INTRODUCTION

Amir is tha largest player in tha game in Philadelphia, but he made a promise to himself that in 10 yrs. whether he had a little or lot he would retire from tha game & hand tha reins over to his 2 young boys Buck & Twist.

Amir is also a successful biz-ness man who just so happens to love 3 women Liz, Paradise & Allisa however, Amir is oblivious that Paradise is really a federal agent.

Paradise aka Agent Sharp is assigned by tha chief to bring Amir down, they have been trying for years, but never had anything to go on Agent Sharp believes she can do what no other agent has been able to do bring Amir down, but unfortunately for her as she spends time wit Amir she finds herself falling deeply in love wit him even compromising her job.

Will love be enough when Amir learns tha truth that Paradise isn't who he thought she was & that she's really a Fed working to bring him down what will he do? Will he accept her explanation & forgive her? Or will he ignore his feelings because tha trust is broken & kill her?

Either way something or someone will be compromised!

# CHAPTER 1

## Agent Sharp Bring This Guy Down

"We've been trying to bring this guy down for years and we still don't have nothing to go off of," tha Chief said to Agent Sharp.

"Chief, if you let me, I'm sure I can get him," said Agent Sharp.

"That's what all tha others said too," he replied.

"Yeah, but they're not me," tha agent quickly responded.

"A'ight, Imma a give you one year to get tha job done."

"Trust me Chief, you won't regret it."

"What ever you need you just let me know Agent Sharp."

"Yes Chief."

"Be careful."

"I will."

# CHAPTER 2

## Tha Big Party

"Amir."

"What up Tex?"

"They say tha boy Cream is having a big party tonight at Club Flo."

"I know, Stylz just hit me."

"You fuckin' wit it?"

"Do Muslims make salat? Imma have to shoot to King of Prussia to grab something to wear."

"You better call Stylz, he was headed there too."

"What about you?"

"I'm cool, I keep some fly shit in tha walk-in."

"I heard that, well I'll hit you up later."

"No doubt."

"Oh yeah, did Aunt Jean's plane land yet?"

"Yeah, she got in early this morning."

"A'ight, I'll call her when I'm done shopping."

"Make sure you do, she's been worried about you."

"Imma call, have you seen Fourty?"

"Yeah, he's wit me."

"Tell him shorty was ask'n bout him."


"Tex told me to tell you shorty was ask'n bout you."

"I'm not surprised tha way I put it on her."

"Nigga, I told you not to knock her off."

"Yeah, and I told you I was grown!"

"All I know is, you better not Fuck it up for us!"

"She's still going to play her position."

"Until you stop fuck'n her."

"Nah, we already established what tha deal is if we stop fuck'n."

"A'ight, I hear you, Imma get a backup just in case."

"Do what ever you feel you need to do."

"Are you going to Cream's party tonight?"

"I don't know, I was thinking about it."

"It's gon' be bitches everywhere."


"What about this Tex?"

"That Shit Hot!"

"I know right."

"I'm try'n to Fuck something strange tonight."

"Me too, I hope Malaya show up tonight."

"You know she'll be in tha building wit Roxy and tha other chick."

"Hopefully she'll stop fronting and get at a nigga."

"You know tha chase is tha best part because once you capture tha prize tha fun and thrill is gone."

"I hope it's worth it, I been try'n to get at her for tha past six months."

"Damn, and you haven't even got her number yet?"

"All that is going to change tonight."

"I've got a feeling you may be right."

"Come on, let's pay for tha stuff and be out."

"Amir said that work came in this morning."

"Now that's what I'm talking about, I've got my people in Delaware on a hold for 10 of them things."

"I think Imma pull tha Maserati out tonight."

"Daaaamn, you pulling out all tha stops to get Mayla ain't you?"

"Nah, if this 'pose to be tha party of all parties I need to come correct."

"You gon' make me pull out my Maybach."

"Go hard or go home is my motto."

"I definitely feel you on that."

"I gotta be at tha shop in an hour."

"Shit let me call Ern, I hope he can squeeze me in."

"You good, I booked us all an appointment."

"What would we do wit out you Tex?"

"Let's hope you'll never find out."

"Mayla how does this dress look on me?"

"Damn Bitch, that's you all day."

"Wow, paradise you must be try'n to catch a big fish tonight?"

"No sense in half stepping."

"I say that's right."

"Mayla, you know ya boy gonna be in tha building."

"Who my boy?"

"Bitch stop frontin', you know damn well who I'm talkin' bout."

"If I knew, I wouldn't have to ask who."

"Tex Bitch!"

"That's not my boy."

"You still try'n to play hard to get, you better stop before somebody else scoops him up."

"I could care less."

"Paradise, you hear this hussy frontin'?"

"Umm Hmm."

"Well damn, who side you on?"

"Family or not, Mayla you frontin' I see tha way you be staring at him."

"What ever."

"You know we right."

"Just cause you wanna get at his boy Amir, don't mean I want Tex."

"You right, but you do want Tex."

"Like I said, "Whaaat Eeever."

"We better get to tha shop y'all know how Casey is when you're not on time."

"Just let me pay for my stuff."

"All them other bitches better have their Shit together tonight."

"Even if they do, they not seeing us, we them bitches."

"I say that's right," Roxy said dapping Mayla.

# CHAPTER 3

## Amir Meets Paradise

"I don't believe we standing in this long ass line."

"Well, had we known you had to have a V.I.P. ticket we wouldn't be standing in this line."

"Oh Shit, God Damn, Holy Shit, Who's Dat?" Were just a few of tha comments as tha four car caravan came cruising alone.

We all looked as they pulled up to tha valet in V.I.P. parking. Tex was tha first to get out his cherry red Maserati followed by Stylz in his black Maybach, then Fourty in his navy-blue Ferrari. And last but not least, Amir hops out his white on white Aston Martin wit a pair of pink Gucci linen pants wit a white V-neck Gucci shirt and pink and white Gucci sneakers. To top it off his wrist, neck, and ears were so icy I caught a chill. Roxy nudged me, when I looked at her she pointed to Mayla who was staring at Tex.

"UNH, UNH, UNH, look at you Ms. I don't like Tex."

"I know you ain't talkin' tha way you was staring at Amir."

"I'm allowed to look."


"Hey Tex, ain't that Mayla in that long ass line?"

"Where?"

"Right there."

"Sure is, let me help them out, hold up y'all."

"How are you doing Ms. Mayla?"

"Hey Tex."

"Why y'all standing in this long ass line looking all fly?"

"We tried to get in V.I.P. but they said we need tickets."

"We don't got no tickets."

"Well, I guess y'all will be in this line wit us."

"Yeah right. Watch, you look like tha betting type. What do you say we make a bet?"

"Depends on what it is."

"If I get us in V.I.P., you let me buy you a drink."

"And if you don't?"

"If I don't, I'll buy you a drink so it's a win win situation."

"Aye Tex bring 'em and come on."

"Come on y'all. Damn, pardon my rudeness what's up Roxy and..."

"Nah," Fourty said.

Amir pulled out a knot of hundreds then said, "Yes we do."

After peeling off 20 of them tha bouncer put a bracelet on all our wrist.

"Paradise, I quickly let him know."

"And Paradise. Tex, Stylz, Fourty, and Amir what's up?"

"We can't call it," they said in unison.

"Y'all got V.I.P. tickets?"

"I guess I owe you a drink," Tex said handing me a 50-dollar bill.

"Nope, you gon' go to tha bar and get it."

"If you insist."

"Mayla who ya girl?"

"That's my cousin and you can ask her ya selfya self."

"Hello, how are you doing?"

"Fine."

"I'm Amir."

"Paradise."

"Not sounding corny or lame, but that name definitely fits you like that dress you're wearing."

I couldn't front Paradise was bad as Hell, 5'6", bronze skin tone, green eyes, pretty shoulder length hair, and an ass that would make tha rapper Trina jealous.

"Can I ask you a question wit out you getting offended?"

"Yes, they're my real eyes."

"I take it you get asked that just as much as you get asked ya number?"

"All tha time."

"Can I buy you a drink?"

"Not to be rude, but I can buy my own drink."

"Listen Shawty, I don't know what type of guys you use to dealing wit but I'm not expecting you to go home wit me for buying you a drink or two."

"Well, in that case, yes you can buy me a drink."

"It's always tha lames that mess it up for good brothers like myself."

"Oh, so you one of tha good ones?"

"I'd like to think so."

"What's ya choice of drink?"

"Cîroc wit a splash of orange juice?"

"Cîroc?"

"Yeah Cîroc."

"I'll be right back."


"That's right Paradise get him."

"Roxy you crazy."

"At least you not frontin'."

"Neither am I."

"What ever Mayla, you could have just took tha money, but no, you wanted him to get tha drink."

"You better worry about Stylz," she said pointing at some chick that was all in his face."

"I don't have to, me and Stylz are just friends."

"Tell that Shit to somebody who might believe you."

"You don't have to, we know what's going on." I was try'n to convince myself more than I was Mayla.

"What up Sexy?"

"You," Roxy said wit all smiles.

"You wit me tonight?"

"You sure you want me and not one of these other broads?"

"I wouldn't have asked if I wasn't sure."

"You two still playing that friend Shit?" Tex asked wit two drinks in his hands.

"Mayla looked at Roxy then said, "I rest my case."

"Please don't get me started Mayla."

*"I BE RIDING THRU MY OLD HOOD BUT I'M IN MY NEW WHIP SAME 'OL ATTITUDE BUT I'M ON SOME NEW SHIT."*

"Yo this my Shit! Come on Stylz."

"They so fake, if they just don't make it official."

"Here you go Ma."

"Paradise."

"My fault."

"That's a major turn off when a guy calls you Ma, Boo, Shawty, or Baby."

"Thanks for tha heads up, I'll remember that for tha next time we're together."

"Next time?"

"Yup."

"How do you know there will be a next time."

"Honestly, I'm hoping to maybe get to know you better."

"That could be a possibility."

"Well, I'll give you my number and if you want to do lunch or dinner, or just have a drink you can call me."

Paradise handed me her I-Phone, so I could store my number.

"I put both my numbers in just in case I don't answer one you can hit me on tha other one."

"A'ight but let me take ya picture."

"For what, you a Fed?"

"Boy no, so I can store it wit ya numbers."

"Just playing, no need to get hostile."

"How would you like it if I asked if you were a snitch?" Tha look on his face said it all.

"Once again, I apologize."

I couldn't front Amir was Sexy as Shit.

Mayla walked up, "Damn, are you going to party or talk to Amir all night?"

"Why is there a problem?" Amir asked before I could say anything.

"Excuse me, I'm going to get my party on."

"Well, hopefully you'll put those numbers to use."

"Now you try'n to get rid of me?"

"Nah, I just don't want to stop you from having fun and mingling."

"How do you know I'm not already having fun."

"I'm just saying, I see all these other niggaz checking you out."

"You know just like I do, all they want is some ass."

"Would you like to join me in V.I.P.?"

"I don't want to cramp ya style."

"You could never do that if anything you'll make my stock go up."

"Boy you crazy."


"Well, Well, if it isn't tha boy Amir."

"What's up Cream?"

"You know M-O-N-E-Y," he said spelling tha word *'money'* out.

"You need to take some of that money and invest it in something legit."

"Why would I do that when I make plenty of doe this way?"

"Because nothing last forever and ery body needs a Plan B."

"Well, this is my Plan A, B, and C."

"WOW, I thought you were a lot smarter than that I guess I was wrong."

"Amir if tha Alphabet Boys come for me they better bring a body bag cause Imma hold court in tha Mafuckin' streets and that's Real Shit!" Once we were seated at a table I ordered a bottle of Rozay.

"Somebody needs to talk some sense into ya boy."

"Excuse me?"

"Ya man you was just talkin' to. Some people let this money blind them."

"And you don't?"

"I don't plan to be in this Shit too much longer, 2 to 3 years tops."

"I'm guessing you have a Plan B?"

"Paradise, I have three biz-nesses that do very well."

"So why not get out now?"

"Tha people I deal wit I promised them I would give them a few more years and I don't break promises." We were so deep into our conversation that neither of us realized what time it was.

"Well Paradise, it was definitely a pleasure to have met you and hopefully I'll get to see you again soon."

"I'm sure you will." We made our way to tha front of tha club where Mayla and Roxy were standing wit Tex, Stylz, and Fourty.

"Damn, y'all decided to join us?"

"Nigga go head, y'all could have joined us in V.I.P.?

"Y'all were so busy talkin' y'all wouldn't have noticed us anyway."

"I'm outta here, it's past my bedtime."

"We were all going to grab a bite to eat."

"I'm good, just get at me in tha a.m."

"How about you Paradise?"

"I think I'll take a pass this time."

"Well, you can take my car since I drove us here?"

"No problem just hit my phone in tha morning."

"Y'all sure y'all don't want to join us?"

"Yeah, I've got to show one of my houses early in tha morning."

"Oh, you're into real estate?"

"I told you I have three biz-nesses."

"I know but you didn't say what they were."

"Maybe when you want to buy a house you can call me."

"That might not be a bad idea since I'm looking to buy another house soon."

"Well, we can talk about that over dinner Friday night."

"I'll have to check my schedule and get back to you."

"You know tha number."


On tha ride home, I couldn't get Paradise off my mind; there was something intriguing about her. It seemed like as soon as I got to sleep my alarm clock was going off. I hit tha snooze, but 10 minutes later it was going off again.

After showering, I decided to throw on a pair of sky-blue Ralph Lauren linen capris, a white V-neck, and all-white Ralph Lauren sneaks. I would stop by Joanne's to pick up a sandwich since I didn't have time to cook. Because I called my order in it was ready when I got there.

"Good morning Ms. Joanne."

"Good morning Amir did my sister ever call you about that house?"

"As a matter of fact, I'm on my way to meet her now."

"Oh well, tell her I said to call me later."

"Will do, you have a good day."

"You do tha same."


15 minutes later, I was pulling up to tha Brownstone on Cecil B. Moore.

"Hello Amir."

"Hello Ms. Liz."

"Runnin' a little late?"

"I know, sorry about that, I was just runnin' my mouth at Ms. Joanne's."

"Trust me, I know how that goes."

"She told me to tell you to call her later."

"A'ight, shall we look at this house now?"

I couldn't front, Ms. Liz was a bad old moms, she put a lot of these young girls to shame, face and body wise. She reminded me of tha actress Vanessa Williams wit tha body of tennis player Serena Williams.

"Your husband didn't come wit you?"

"My husband?"

"Yeah, tha guy that was wit you tha last time we met."

"Oh No Honey, that was my vocal teacher, I had to pick him up, but you called so I made him ride wit me."

"He didn't look like somebody you would marry anyway."

"Honey I'm 42 and he can't do nothing for me, I need a young stallion to keep up wit me," she said winking. *She better be careful, I might have her bent over in one of these rooms,"* I thought to myself.

"Wow, this place is lovely; how much is this going to cost me?"

"Depends."

"On what?"

"If you want to rent or buy."

"Does it come wit tha option to mortgage?"

"Of course."

"Well, I'll take it then."

"A'ight, we can go to my office to do tha paperwork."

"One more question."

"Yes?"

"Does it come wit all this furniture?"

"I told you it was fully furnished unless you have your own stuff you want to put in?"

"No, no, I love it just tha way it is, especially tha master bedroom," she said winking again. I couldn't help but smile.

"Listen Amir, let me be upfront wit you, I want to Fuck you right here right now."

"That sounds good, but I don't want it to interfere wit biz-ness."

"Believe me it won't and if you're any good, you'll get tha pleasure of getting some more of this," she said dropping her Chanel dress to tha floor revealing her naked body that was flawless.

"What's tha matter? Cat got ya tongue?"

Wit out saying anything, I walked up to her and picked her up carrying her to tha bedroom. Once my clothes were off it was on, Liz tried to take control. I quickly let her know I was no New Jack.


One hour and five orgasms later we were both in tha shower.

"Damn, I truly underestimated you Amir."

"They all do, I may be 20 but I can handle my own."

"Yes you can."

"I've been wit a lot of broads, but you are by far tha best."

"Does that mean I'll be seeing you again?"

"That's up to you."

"I don't want to overstep my boundaries."

"I'll let you know if and when you do."

"What do you say we go another round?"

"My thoughts exactly."

"I could get use to this."

"So could I, it's been a loooong time since I've been able to have that many orgasms wit out using my toys."

"Liz that was just a warm up for me."

"Awe Shit let's go again unless you have some place you need to be?"

"Not at all."

For tha rest of tha day we laid up only stopping to catch our breath. Liz taught me a few new things and vice versa.

# CHAPTER 4

## One Down, Two to Go

For tha next few days me and Liz went at it like two lovers.

"Whoooa! It just gets better and better every time."

"I have to handle some biz-ness, I'll hit you up later or should I just swing by?"

"You already know what I'm going to say."

"I will call you before I come just in case you have company."

She gave me that look that said yeah right. I watched as Liz got up and walked into tha bathroom ass bouncing.

*Umm, Umm, Umm, let me get outta here before I be up in that again,"* I said to myself.

"Liz, I'll be back later."

"A'ight, don't eat, Imma cook something." I thought Ms. Joanne could cook but she ain't got nothing on Liz.


When I pulled up to tha block, Fourty, Stylz, and Tex were all sitting on tha green box.

"What up stranger?"

"What up y'all?"

"We don't know, you tell us, you tha one been M.I.A. in tha past few days."

"I told y'all I been chillin' wit Liz."

"Damn, old moms must have a Hell of a shot."

"I can't front, she definitely got it going on."

"Let me find out she got my boy Fucked up."

"I wouldn't go that far."

"So what's up wit Paradise?"

"I don't know? She never called me."

"She try'n to play hard like Mayla was."

"Did I hear you right?"

"Yup, I threw this good wood on her, she can't stop calling now."

(Tha phone rings)

*"DON'T WANNA FUCK UP YA PANTIES BETTER TAKE 'EM OFF."*

"Speak of tha Devil…Hello."

"Amir, did you hit Mike-Mike off wit that work yet?"

"Nah, I ain't did Shit in tha past few days that's why I came out today to take care of biz-ness."

"Well, that would explain why he been calling my phone all crazy."

"You didn't hit him off?"

"I haven't even answered his calls because I thought his sister told him to call me."

"You not still Fuckin' that crazy chick, are you?"

"Hell No!"

"I was about to say you playing wit that girl feelings by keep knocking her down."

"She got some bomb head and pussy, just can't deal wit all tha drama that comes wit it."


"Aye Stylz, you try'n to go to tha movies later?"

"Nah."

"I told Mayla I didn't want to go either, but she told me to ask you and call back."

"I ain't messing wit them, I got other shit set up."

"That's all it is then, let me hit her back right now so she won't cancel her plans if she had any."


"Amir, I got this sweet weed Connect out of Cali."

"Yeah."

"Yeah, 450 a pound, but if they bring it all tha way it's an extra 50 dollars a pound."

"500 a pound, is tha weed any good?"

"You tell me," Fourty said handing me a Dutch already rolled up.

"Light it up."

I took a couple pulls, held it then blew tha smoke out. After a few more pulls I was high as Hell.

"Damn, this must be some Exotic."

"Nigga that shit regular."

"Get tha Fuck Outta Here."

"That's tha same thing I said when he let me try it."

"You need to get up wit ya man A.S.A.P."

"I wanted to make sure we were all on board."

"You got some more?"

"Yeah, he gave me a couple pounds to check out."

"I need some."

"I got you, I just gotta grab it from Shorty's."

"Let's grab a 100 to see how it moves."

"Imma hit Lil' Dave and bone off on Clearfield."

"You try'n to break it down."

"Damn Right, tha flip will be serious."

"Yeah, but we don't want to be sittin' on a 100 pounds for weeks."

"Trust me, we won't."

"A'ight, we'll see."


"There that nigga go over there."

"You sure you want to do this wit all these people out here?"

"It's not like they gonna know who we are thanks to ya man."

"Oh yeah, I forgot all about these."

"Come on, let's get him."


"Old timers, I got that Drag Net," I motioned for him to come over, "how many you want?"

"How many can you handle?"

"I don't have time for games."

"I ain't playing no games," I said pulling out a wad of cash.

"Follow me then."

"Rex where you going?" Some broad yelled from across tha street.

"I'll be right back."

We followed him into this ally. Before either of us realized what was going Rex pulled out a knife.

"A'ight, run that paper Old Heads."

"Listen Youngin', I think you might wanna reconsider this."

"Nah, I think y'all better give that cash up."

He never knew what hit him. "PIT, PIT, PIT...PIT, PIT, PIT."

We both caught him three times in tha chest. We walked out in tha opposite direction we came in. One down two to go.


"Hello."

"What up Main Man?"

"Damn Big Homey, I been try'n to get in touch wit you. I even Tried to call Stylz, but he didn't answer either."

"He told me he thought you were calling for your sister."

"Ha Ha! Ha! I told him not to mess wit that dizzy bitch!"

"Ain't she ya sister?"

"She still dizzy and I tried to warn him. Sometimes a pretty face and a fat butt will make you think wit tha wrong head.

"Yeah, I know how that is."

"I bet you do, so what's up?"

"I need to see you A.S.A.P."

"Tha usual?"

"Double it up for me."

"A'ight, plus I'll front you another ten."

"That's good shit."

"Come on, you know you my peoples, I gotta make sure you straight."

"You always do."

"Same spot 20 minutes."

"No problem."


"Amir, you want me to ride wit you?"

"If you want, it don't matter. Fourty, Stylz hold it down we bout to make a run." My phone started going off, but I didn't know tha number, so I didn't answer it.

Two minutes later, tha same number popped up.

"Yo who dis?"

"Is that how you answer ya phone?"

"It is when I don't know tha number."

"Well, you might need to stop giving ya number out so much."

"That's tha problem, I don't."

"Well if that's tha case, you should know who calls ya phone."

"Listen, I'm not going to sit here and go back-and-forth, so who is this and what can I do for you?"

"Excuse me smart ass."

"I'm not try'n to be smart."

"Well in that case, it's Paradise."

"Oh Shit, it's been a few weeks, I thought you forgot about a nigga."

"I do have a job, plus I didn't want to seem thirsty."

"Any excuse is better than none."

"No excuse just tha truth."

"I hear that."

"Are you busy?"

"Not really, on my way to collect some rent."

"Is that ya way of saying you're doing a drug transaction?"

"Nah, I told you I own some real estate."

"Oh yeah you did."

"Would you like to get together later for a few drinks?"

"That's sounds good."

"OK I'll call you in a few hours."


"Damn, who was that tha Feds?"

"Nah, but she act like it."

"Ya old moms?"

"Nah Paradise."

"You didn't tap that yet?"

"No, that was tha first time we talked since that night."

"Oh, she's another Mayla."

"I don't know? There's something about her I don't trust."

"Don't deal wit her."

"Imma knock her down first then cut her off."

"As you should."

"So, you gonna make Mayla wifey?"

"I don't know, I kinda like being a male whore."

"You don't have to stop."

"I know but I'll have to sneak around and I'm not for that. Imma just sit back and enjoy tha ride."

"Hey, ride it til tha wheels fall off."

"Why would I do anything else?"


As we were pulling up to meet Mike-Mike I saw tha nigga Shaft that owed me some loot from tha basketball game.

"Yo Shaft what up Playboy?

"Damn Nigga, I was starting to think you didn't want ya doe."

"Nah, I knew you was good for it, besides is only 5 g's."

"I respect that, I'll be right back."

While I was doing that, Tex had already took care of biz-ness wit Mike-Mike.

"He said he'll hit you when he's ready. What's up wit Shaft?"

"Nothing, he just went to grab some doe he owed me from a bet."

Two minutes later, some bad ass chick walked up.

"Which one of y'all is Amir?"

"Why?"

"Shaft told me to give you this," she said pulling out tha money.

"I am," I answered after seeing tha money, "tell him next time don't send his girl.

"His girl? Boy pleeeease, that's my brother.

"Oh my bag Shorty."

"My name is Allisa not Shorty."

"I didn't mean no disrespect."

"It's cool, well y'all be safe."

"You too." When she turned to leave I was speechless.

"Allisa."

"Yes."

"You forgot something."

"What did I forget?"

"My number."

"Oh did I?"

"You sure did."

"How about I give you my number and you can call me if you really want to talk."

"That'll work."

"If you're not going to call me don't ask for my number."

"I would've never tried to give you my number if I wasn't interested."

"We'll see."

"Matter fact, if you're not busy how bout dinner later?"

"That works for me."

"I'll call you around 8 o'clock."

This time when she turned to walk away she put a little extra bounce in her walk.

"Damn Amir, that might be too much for you."

"I doubt that my nigga."

# CHAPTER 5

## Agent Sharp Build a Case on Amir Miles

"What have you got for me Agent Sharp?"

"Nothing yet but I'll have something real soon Chief."

"I can see that you're not going to have any luck on this case."

"Chief, I've only been on this case for 60 days a case like this takes time."

"Well, you only have 10 months left."

"Chief, I may need a little more time."

"Agent Sharp I gave you one year."

"I know but it's gonna take that much time just to get next to him and get him to trust me."

"You just build me a case in tha next 10 months and we'll go from there, understood?"

"Yes Chief."

"Now get outta here and build a case on Amir Miles."

"I'll bet my life on it."

# CHAPTER 6

## Paradise Calls Amir

"Hello."

"Hey there You."

"Who Dis?"

"Who do you want it to be?"

"I'm sorry but I don't have time to play tha guessing game."

"It's me, Paradise."

"If you call more maybe I would know ya voice."

"Ouch. I guess I deserve that."

"Let me be up front wit you and if you hang up and never call back, so be it."

"I'm listening."

"All this cat and mouse Bullshit is not me, so if you want to continue playing games I highly suggest you find another nigga to play wit!"

I couldn't believe Amir just talked to me like that, but for some strange reason it turned me on to tha point my panties were actually moist.

"I feel what you're saying and you're right, so maybe we can do dinner tonight?"

"I'm not going to be able to do that I have a prior engagement; maybe we can do lunch or dinner tomorrow."

"What ever works for you I'm on ya time now."

"It ain't like that."

"You got my number jus call me." She hung up before I could respond. I could tell she was pissed, but I didn't care one bit.

"You and Liz on tha outs?"

"Nah, that was Paradise. She want me to sweat her I guess, but I don't do that."

"Sounds like Mayla, then once you get her she's hooked like a fish."

"So, you got her chasing you now?"

"Chasing? More like stalking."

"Nigga you like that shit."

"Truth be told, I do cause I'm giving her a taste of her own medicine."

"You two were made for each other."

"Why is that?"

"You just are."


"Did you talk to ya uncle yet?"

"Nah, Imma get wit him today."

"Man, you been saying that for a minute now."

"I know, that's because I didn't want him to know I was hustling."

"Yeah but his team is winning, and they got tha best work in tha city, hands down."

"I know, that's why Imma definitely get at him today."

"Oh Shit!"

"What's up?"

"Look across tha street."

I turned to look, and a big smile instantly came across my face.

"Well, Well, Well, he finally came outta hiding."

"Come on let's get this nigga."

"Hold up Twist, just be patient."

"I ain't trying to let this nigga get away."

"Trust me, he ain't gon' get away."

"My uncle told me I needed to be more discrete about tha way I do things."

"Nigga we respected in this town. How you think you got tha name Buck?"

"My uncle gave me tha name Buck Wild when I was three, but as I got older he dropped tha Wild and been calling me Buck ever since."

"Nigga you only 15, you make it sound like you 30-years-old or something."

"Come on let's follow him."


After following him for 30 minutes he pulled up to a motel.

"Pull over right here."

"Why?"

"I don't want him to see us."

"A'ight, just make sure you see what room he goes in."

Once he was in tha room I had Twist pull around to tha back, so our car wouldn't be spotted.

"Hand me that outta tha glove box."

"You come prepared, don't you?"

"No need to wake tha neighbors."

"Come on let's do this." (KNOCK, KNOCK)

"Who is it?"

"Pizza delivery."

"I didn't order no pizza."

"You sure, this is tha room number?"

"Hold on." I could hear him moving some stuff around.

"How much do I owe you?" he asked opening up tha door only to be met by my .45 in his face.

"What tha Fuck is going on?"

"Shut up Nigga, back up!"

"Listen, that beef we had is over."

"Nah my nigga, how can it be over when my little homey is in a box. It's a life for a life. Actually, in this case, a life for three," tha look on his face said it all, "that's right Nigga, that was us that did ya boy Rex. Now you then Spinx."

"Hold on Buck, I got a proposition for this nigga."

"Ain't no proposition gon' save his life."

"Chaz, how much ya life worth to you?"

"I can give you a 100 grand."

"Where is it?"

"I have it go get it."

"Wrong answer."

"Let me make a call."

"Does it look like we're stupid?"

"How else are you gon' get it?"

"We'll just take what you have in this room."

"I don't have Shit in here."

"You're not a very good liar."

"Twist tear this Mafucka up."

Tha look on Chaz face let me know we'd find something and sure enough, Twist came out tha bathroom wit a duffel bag.

"Buck, I wonder what's in here."

Once Twist dumped tha contents on tha bed, I did everything in my power not to smile.

"Yo that's not mine."

"It's in ya room."

"My plug is gonna kill me."

"Oh yeah? Well, you don't have to worry about that I'm gon' save him tha trouble." (PIT, PIT, PIT, PIT, PIT) Five shots tha chest and one (PIT) to tha head.

"Buck this about 5 bricks and 60 grand."

"Only way to go from here is up."

"Ain't no stoppin' us now."

"Once we get rid of this we can step to my unc wit a nice piece of change."

"We got Rex and Chaz, now all we need to do is find Spinx."

"We'll get his bitch ass, don't worry."


(AMIR CALLS PARADISE)

"Hello."

"Hey, do you have any plans for lunch?"

"Actually, me, Mayla, and Roxy were about to get a bite."

"Oh, OK. Hit me up later on then."

"I can always have lunch wit them, who knows when I'll get another opportunity to have lunch wit tha infamous Amir."

"So, I'll take that as a yes."

"Yes."

"Be ready in 30 minutes."

30 minutes later, Amir was calling my phone to say he was pulling up.

"Bye Bitches," I said to Mayla and Roxy as I was heading for tha door.

"Don't get knocked up."

"Yeah right, we only going to lunch."

"I'm just saying."

"Fuck you Mayla."

"No thanks, Tex is doing a fine job of that." We all busted out laughing as I headed out tha door.

"Damn, I thought I was going to have to call you again."

"My fault, Mayla and Roxy had jokes."

"I bet they did. What do you have a taste for?"

"I could give my right hand for some shrimp."

"You sure you wanna loose ya right hand for some shrimp?"

"It's just a figure of speech."

"I know this seafood place in Mount Airy that's off tha chain."

"Let's go then."

20 minutes later, we were in front of "All About Seafood."

"I heard about this place."

"Well, you should know they have tha best shrimp in town maybe tha world for that matter." Once we were inside tha restaurant we were seated by a waitress.

"Can I get you anything to drink while you look over your menu?"

"I'll have a Coke."

"And you Sir."

"Bottled Spring Water."

"A'ight, I'll be right back."

"Don't worry about tha price."

"I was always told if a menu doesn't have prices it usually means it's expensive."

"Like I said, don't worry about tha prices."

"I think I want tha Shrimp Delight." Once tha waitress came back we both placed our orders.

"Will that be all?"

"Yes."


"So Paradise, if you don't mind me asking where do you work?"

"I work for a law firm."

"A lawyer huh?"

"Not criminal, civil."

"Oh so, you get people money?"

"I try to."

"If you don't mind me asking, what other biz-ness do you own besides property?" Paradise asked.

"I have a cleaning service and I own a corner store."

"You're not worried that they might take any of them?"

"They can't."

"You obtained them wit drug money."

"That's where your wrong, my pop-pop passed away and left me a hefty piece of money, so I did what any smart person who has money would do, invest."

"I'm not tha police, you don't have to lie to me."

"I know, all my stuff is documented."

"So tha Feds can't touch them?"

For some reason it felt like Paradise was fishing, but for what I don't know. Our waitress came back at tha perfect time.

"Shrimp Delight for you and tha Crab Special for you."

"Thank you."

"You're welcome, if you need anything else please let me know."

"Will do."


"How much do you want for a bird?"

"Where did that come from?"

"My cousin asked me if I knew anybody wit some good work."

"So, you assumed I would have it?"

"I know that y'all control 80% of tha city."

"I don't know where you get ya info, but you couldn't be more wrong."

"I'm sure you could point me in tha right direction."

"I'm not sure I can."

"Well, if you change your mind he wants 5 bricks."

*I had to laugh to myself, she must think I'm pressed for money.*

"I wish I could help you, but I can't."

"If you say so."

"What's that suppose to mean?"

"Nothing, I just can't believe you gon' let 120 grand get away."

*Damn, this nigga must really be getting paper to let 5 bricks go by. Now I'm starting to see how and why he's never been arrested,"* she thought to herself.

"Thank you for lunch today."

"It ain't about nothing."

"Maybe we can do it again soon."

"You got plans for dinner?"

"I do now."

"Cool, I'll pick you up around 9 o'clock."

"OK, Imma take you to this upscale place so come correct."

"I always do, you don't have to worry about that."

"Tell them you straight, they don't have to check up on you." I turned to see Mayla and Roxy staring out tha window.

"You know how that goes."

"Nah, actually I don't, me and my boys don't do that."

"I know, y'all just talk about all tha bitches y'all Fuck."

"Lame niggaz do shit like that which you must be use to dealing wit."

"Boy let me get out this car before I cuss you out."

"See you at 9."

"Yeah what ever."

"Damn, did I hit a nerve?"

"See you at 9," I said slamming his car door.

# CHAPTER 7

## Amir Makes Love to Liz & Paradise

"Oh My God, this hit is tha bomb It gets better and better every time."

"I aim to please."

"Yes, you sure do. Amir, I think that we may have to end this."

"I thought we had something good going on here?"

"Tha last six months have been tha best, but I told you that if I started catching feelings I would fall back."

Tha funny thing is, I was falling for Liz also, but I wouldn't dare tell her that.

"Well, if you think that's tha best thing to do then I guess it is what it is."

"You don't need no old lady like me catching any feelings cramping ya style."

"If I may say something."

"Sure you can."

"I like what we got going on."

"Don't get me wrong so do I, it's just my feelings are a little involved."

"Ain't nothing wrong wit catching feelings as long as you know how to keep them in check."

"Hmm, I never looked or thought about it like that. So, you wouldn't have a problem wit me having feelings for you?"

"Nah, as long as you can control them."

"I could tell you I could, but truth is I don't know how I would act."

"But I do know I'm no young girl, so all that scratching up cars, bleaching clothes, and running up on tha block is not an option for me.

"Then we're on tha right path already."

"Liz I'm willing to let this play out if you are."

"As long as nothing changes."

"Deal, do we need to shake on it."

"Ha! Ha! Ha! Boy you crazy as Hell."

I was staying wit Liz at least four nights a week anyway so, it was all good. Even though Liz had me by 22 years, I could actually see myself being wit her but tha real question is can I leave all my other broads alone?


"Aye Fourty."

"What up Stylz?"

"I hear Buck and Twist got they little block jumping."

"My sis just asked me if I have given Buck some work because he had a safe in his room."

"What was in it?"

"She didn't look in it she figured it was some work or money that I had given him."

"Them little niggaz 15, it was only a matter of time before they tried their hand."

"I wonder where they getting their work."

"Us."

"You serving them?"

"Naw, but somebody we serving probably is."

"Damn, I never thought about that."

"I wish he would just come to me."

"He probably don't want you to know he's hustling."

"Yeah, I'll let him come to me when he's ready."

"It'll probably be soon once he gets tired of paying those high ass prices."

"Come on let's swing through there."


10 minutes later, we were pulling up on their block.

"Wow look at this traffic moving through here."

"Damn, that little nigga don't look no more than 11-years-old."

"Aye Buck."

"Oh Shit Twist, ain't that my unc?"

"Yup wit my cousin come on let's see what they want."

"Yo what up Unc?"

"Damn, I see somebody turned tha heat up on this block."

"Yeah, my peoples Strap."

"Let me guess, y'all tha sons?"

"And you know it," Twist said while dapping Buck."

"How old is them little niggaz?"

"10, 11, and 13."

"Yeah Unc, they get caught they only gon' get probation."

"Unless they tell."

"They ain't doin' no telling."

"You sure about that?"

"Positive Unc."

"Well a'ight, hit me up if you need me."

"No doubt, no doubt."

"Twist where ya man Strap?"

"He stepped off."

"Why?"

"I wanted to see how much he was getting his work for."

"I could be wrong, but I think $28,000."

"Tell him to holla at us when he ready to re-up."

"Yeah, cause that number is too high."

"A'ight we'll make sure we do that."

"Oh yeah, I almost forgot my whole reason for coming down here."

"What's that?"

"Ya mom said something about a safe in ya room."

"She always worrying, that ain't nothing but some paper I been stacking up."

"Now I know you two niggaz ain't still on that bullshit?"

"Nah Unc, we getting this paper for holding Strap down."

"Like I said, hit me if you need me."

"Always do."


"Yo Fourty, them little niggaz is finally learning."

"I can't believe a Mafucka charging them $28,000 for a brick."

"Even though they probably will see double that breaking it down that number is definitely too high."

"I have a funny feeling Strap will be sending Buck and Twist to get at us when that work is done."

"Them little niggaz is smart to use young boys as long as if something goes down they hold their tongue."

"Hello."

"Yo."

"You sound like you sleep."

"Not really just relaxing."

"Do you want me to call you later?"

"I just told you I wasn't sleep."

"No need to get mad."

"Nobody getting mad, that's ya shit."

"So why haven't you called me?"

"Same reason you haven't called me."

"I just called you, didn't I?"

"Well, what's tha problem then?"

"You're too much."

"No, I'm not, but on a more serious note I've been real busy wit work."

"You could've at least sent me a text or something."

"You know I don't do that texting shit."

"You better get wit tha program; people are doing more texting then they do calling."

"I guess I'll be one of tha ones who still calls."

"It's called new age technology, you better get wit it."

"Only people doing that shit is broads."

"What ever, ya boy Tex do it."

"That's him and what he eat don't make me shit."

"Do you always have to be so Damn smart? Never mind, don't answer that."

"I know you didn't call just to be sarcastic?"

"Actually, I was calling to see if I could treat you to lunch today?"

"Did I just hear you correctly?"

"Yes you did."

"Wow."

"Amir it's not always about you treating me."

"I never said that it was."

"Oh God I feel a but coming."

"But as a man that's what I should be doing."

"Yeah, Yeah. Do you want to do lunch or not?"

"Not."

"Fine."

"Only because I have to meet a client."

"He can wait, those drugs ain't going nowhere."

"This ain't got nothing to do wit no drugs! I told you I don't be dealing wit tha game like that."

"I truly apologize."

"As you should, I'm available for dinner if you don't have any plans later."

"I'll need to check my schedule."

"What ever works for you."

"Boy I'm just kidding, of course I'm available."

"A'ight give me a call when you ready to pick me up."

"Make sure you dress upscale."

"It ain't bout nothing."

"I'm sure it's not, just be ready by 7:30." She hung up before I could repond.

It was close to 7:30 and I hadn't heard from Paradise yet. Right when I was about to change my clothes my phone rang.

"Hello."

"I detect a little attitude."

"It's after 7:30."

"I'm sorry, I got held up in a meeting at tha office."

"Well, you should have called, if there is one thing I hate is somebody being late."

"Look, I said I was sorry and I'm out front if you still want to go."

I had to admit Amir was looking good in his cream Gucci suit, brown shirt wit his cream and brown Gucci loafers to match.

"You sure do know how to throw it on."

"Thank you."

"You're more than welcome."

"They say great minds think alike," I said referring to her brown Dior dress and cream shoes.

"I know, look at us looking like a couple."

"That's not a bad thing."

"That depends on who you ask."

"What's that supposed to mean?"

"According to tha critics I'm a gold digger and you're too good for me."

"As long as you and I know tha deal then nothing else matters."

"I know but I don't want that label cause like Webby say I'm I-N-D-E-P-E-N-D-E-N-T, got my own car, my own cash."

"Ha! Ha! Ha! You funny as Hell."

"Is that why you wanted to treat me to dinner tonight?"

"Not at all, I just want you to know it's OK for me to foot tha bill."

"If you don't mind me asking, where are we going?"

"To this spot in Wilmington."

"You must be talking about tha Hotel DuPont."

"Is there anywhere you haven't been?"

"Probably not."

It's been five months and Paradise still hasn't given up tha goods as of yet, not that I really tried.

"What are you doing?"

"I'm parking."

"Not here, pull up to valet."

"I don't like to use valet."

"Why not?"

"I just don't trust 'em."

"Well, you don't have to worry about that tonight." She reluctantly pulled up to valet.

"Good evening."

"Oh, what up Amir?"

"I can't call it."

"I ain't seen you in a while."

"Busy wit work, you know how that goes."

"My aunt loves tha crib you sold her."

"I told her she would."

"Where are my boys?"

"They off tonight."

"Take care of my peoples' wheels," I said handing him a crisp c-note.

"I always do."

"No doubt."


"Hello Mr. Adams, do you have reservations?"

"No, he doesn't but I do."

"I'm sorry your name?"

"Miller."

"Oh yes here you are, this way please."

Tha hostess escorted us to a private table for two.

"Is there anybody here that doesn't know you?"

"I doubt it."

"Wow, they have not a lot of good things on tha menu."

"Like you've never been here before."

"I haven't, one of my coworkers told me about it."

"I suggest you try tha Teriyaki steak and shrimp."

"It better be good."

"Trust me, once you try it you'll never eat anything else from off that menu."

"Have you ever tried anything else?"

"Of course, but once I had this I didn't want anything else."

"Are you guys ready to order or do you need more time?"

"Betty, I got this one, go take ya break. Hey Amir."

"Hey Tanya."

"I already know what you want Amir, what can I get for you Mam?"

"I'll have what he's having."

"Will that be all?"

"Bring me a bottle of Chardonnay."

"A'ight, I'll be right back."

"Don't worry I'll pay for that."

"Now you disrespecting me."

"Nah, tha bottle I get is expensive." We both sipped on tha champagne while we talked and waited for our meal.


"Wow, that was delicious."

"I told you that you would love it."

"I'm so full right now it don't make no sense."

"You look like you put on 5 pounds."

"I see you got jokes, Amir do you have something to do in tha morning?"

"Nah."

"Well, I was thinking maybe we could get a room here and just chill for tha night."

In my mind I was thinking Oh Hell No, but my mouth said sure why not. Every time we stay wit each other all we did was cuddle. Let me call my man to see if he has some weed for me since it's going to be a long night. "I need to use your car while you get a room."

"Sure, go ahead, I'll call you wit tha room number."

"Works for me."

"Before you go, let me get my overnight bag out of there."


30 minutes later, I was back knocking on tha room door.

"I thought you went back to Philly?" Paradise said standing in her sexy lingerie."

*"I should've,"* I thought to myself.

"What you smiling for?"

"Just admiring tha artwork."

"Oh, so now I'm a piece of artwork?"

"Yup, priceless."

"You got more game then tha Green Bay Packers."

"What you know about tha Packers?"

"What Boy that's my squad. Who's ya team?"

"You won't believe me if I told you."

"Try me."

"Imma a diehard Packers fan, been to more games that I can count. I even went to tha Super Bowl in Dallas when we bust tha Steelers ass."

"On that note, I need a glass of champagne, pour me a shot of Bombay while I twist this up please."

"Only because you said please."

"Amir let me ask you something."

"Shoot."

"You're a hustler, right?"

"Go on."

"Well, why don't you get this money?"

"Excuse me."

"For tha past few months my cousin has been trying to score from you, but you won't deal wit him."

"Listen Paradise, no disrespect to you but I don't know your cousin."

"But you do know me."

"Do I?"

"What's that suppose to mean?"

"Do I really know you?"

"We been talking for five months and two of those you were playing games."

"For all I know, you could be this pretty chick working undercover to book me."

"Mafucka I ain't no Fuckin cop! Forgive me for trying to hook my cousin up and put some money in ya pocket."

"I don't need no money, I'm crazy straight."

"For tha record, this is tha second time you've called me tha police, there will not be a third!"

"I'm just not use to a female coming at me about no drugs."

"If tha shoe was on tha other foot I would hope you would try to do tha same."

"Don't get me wrong, I definitely respect you I'm just not into dealing wit new people."

"Then turn him on to one of your boys."

"Nah, I wouldn't put them in that type of situation."

"What situation?"

"For all I know, ya cousin could be working wit tha law."

"So, you think I would do that to you?"

"Paradise, you wouldn't know if he was a snake."

"We're close."

"I understand but at tha end of tha day you're not wit him 24-7 so you don't know what he's into."

"You're so right but I do trust him."

"Tha keywords in that sentence was you trust him."

"I need another glass."

"Me too," I said handing her my glass.

She just looked at me.

"Please."

"That's better."

After a few more shots, I was a little horny, but I knew that Paradise wouldn't be giving me sex, so I rolled another blunt.

"Amir, you should stop smoking that stuff."

"This shit is good for you."

"No, it's not."

"If that was true they wouldn't have legalized it."

"They didn't."

"What do you call medical marijuana?"

"That's for medical purposes."

"It's helping Mafuckas."

"Yeah, but that's different."

"How is it different?" *I can't wait to hear this.*

"I don't know but it is."

"I rest my case."


I dozed off but was waking by Paradise kissing my face.

"What time is it?"

"10 o'clock."

"In tha morning?"

"Of course not, you wasn't sleep that long."

"I need to smoke."

"Imma jump in tha shower while you do that."

I couldn't help but to watch her walk into tha bathroom ass bouncing. By tha time I finished tha blunt I was smoking, Paradise came strolling out tha bathroom naked wit out a care in tha world.

"If you don't close ya mouth before something flies into it."

"Wow, you are flawless, I think you need to put something on."

"Why?"

"Just because."

Instead of putting my clothes on, I straddled him while putting my tongue in his mouth.

"Paradise, we know how this is going to end and I would rather not travel this road tonight."

I ignored him and kept kissing his chest. If I was going to gain his trust, then it was time to take it to tha next level and that meant doing whatever it took.


"UMM DAMN AAH."

I couldn't believe Paradise was actually giving me head. I knew there was no turning back, so I just went all out.

"You like that Daddy; does it feel good?"

I didn't want to hurt her feelings by saying tha head was trash, so I lied telling her it felt good. I hope tha sex is better than tha head because if not, she won't have to worry about me anymore. I played wit her titties while she finished doing her thing. When she finally came up she wanted me to return tha favor, but I quickly let know that wasn't my thing.

"Well put this on and fuck me," she said wit an attitude.

"It's nothing personal, I just don't go down town."

"A'ight just Fuck me." I slid tha condom on and started giving her tha biz-ness.

"OOOOH SHIT!!! YES! Right there that's my Spot! Oh My God!! What are you doing to me! I'M BOUT TO CUM!!! Her whole body started shaking like she was having a seizure.

"Shit! Shit! Shit! Don't Stop Fuck Me Amir! Give it ALL to Me!

Two minutes later, she was having multiple orgasms back to back. I couldn't believe Amir was hitting it as good as he was. I've never had any man Fuck me like that, in fact, it's not often I have orgasms let alone eight of them.

Five minutes later, I was knocked out.

# CHAPTER 8

## All Night wit Paradise

"I heard you stayed out all night wit Paradise."

"Mayla always runnin' her mouth."

"Let me guess, she still playing?"

"Tex would you believe she gave me some head?"

"Paradise? Nah you Bullshittin'."

"Seriously."

"Was it worth tha wait?"

"Hell Naw, tha head was trash."

"It must run in tha family."

"I can't front, tha shot was good."

"Good enough to stop dealing wit Liz?"

"Hell No! She ain't got nothing on my baby."

"Oh, so now she ya baby?"

"You know that's my folk."

"Nah Nigga you said ya baby."

"She is, she make sure a nigga is crazy straight."

"I bet she does."

"How many of ya broads cook, clean, take ya clothes to tha cleaners, and sex you all crazy?"

"Point taken. I remember you telling me that she was catching feelings."

"That's what she told me."

"If you ask me it's going both ways."

"I'm not saying I'm in love wit her because I'm not, but I do care for her."

"Nigga I'll give you a few more months."

"What ever Nigga."

"All Imma say is I told you so."

"Tex has Mayla said anything about a cousin of hers wanting to cop?"

"No why?"

"Paradise keep trying to get me to deal wit her cousin."

"He must be trying to spend some bread."

"Five birds."

"Is he tha police?"

"That's what I asked, of course she said he wasn't."

"She don't know that."

"I also said that too."

"I'm telling you Tex if I didn't know any better I'd think she was tha law."

"Amir that broad ain't no cop."

"I know but sometimes it just seems like she be fishing."

"All broads are nosey, you know that."


"Yo Buck we gon' need to holla at Fourty."

"We'll just tell him Strap wanted us to get at them."

"Man, he gonna wanna meet him."

"So, we'll take Strap wit us just in case."

"Nah, Nah, if he wants to meet him then we'll bring him."

"A'ight make tha call." After 4 rings he picked up.

"What up Nephew?"

"My peoples trying to score."

"We'll come holla at me, I don't wanna talk over tha phone."

"Where are you?"

"Around tha way."

"Be there in less than 30 minutes."


When we pulled up Tex, Stylz, and my Uncle Fourty were out there.

"Well, Well, Well, if it ain't tha two wildest little niggaz in Philly."

"We ain't on that Ra Ra Shit no more. Unless a Mafucka force our hands."

"That's what I'm talking bout. So, where ya man at?"

"We thought it would be better if everything went through us."

"I'm cool wit that."

"So what numbers lookin' like?"

"For you or him?"

"Us, you know we gotta make something off it."

"21,000."

"If we charge him $24,000 we stand to make $15,000, that's $7,500 apiece." They all looked at one another.

"So, he want 5 birds."

"Yup."

"Well, if that's what he wants he can get 'em for $20,000."

"That's even better, how long will it take to get it?"

"Not long."

"Tha money is in tha trunk."

"Unc make it that thing thing."

"Now you being disrespectful that's all we put out is top notch work."

"If you little niggaz getting six then you ain't making nothing."

"Shit we gon' make $30,000."

"How by selling it?"

"Hell nah, y'all fronted him one for $30,000."

"You two little niggaz gon' make me proud yet." Fourty made a call while we were talking to Amir.

"A'ight Nephew y'all be safe driving back across town."

"You gon' bring it to us?"

"Nah it's already in ya car in tha back seat."

"Damn Unc that's what I'm talkin' bout."

"Y'all just be safe and tell ya man to get back at us when he finished wit that. Hopefully, it won't take him that long to get rid of 'em."

"Tha way that block was jumpin' I doubt it."

"A'ight we'll get up."


"You know that work is for them, don't you?"

"Yeah that's why they got it for that number."

"They caught a nice sting."

"I just hope it doesn't come back on 'em."

"I'm sure they tied up any and all loose ends."

"This is gonna have them on some chill shit."

"I'm not going to front, they got their block jumping'."

"So, check this out, tha new shipment came in this morning so ery body can pick up their share."

"Fourty what up wit that weed?"

"I told you it came in yesterday."

"No you didn't."

"Yeah I did, you probably was too busy wit Liz."

"Oh Shit, you did tell me that, my bag you try to remember something while you in tha middle of something some good head."

"Ha! Ha! Ha! I feel you on that," Tex said dappin' me.

"Are y'all messing wit that Diva's and Bosses party?"

"Damn when is it?"

"Saturday."

"That's three days."

"Imma take a trip up New York for this one."

"We all are."

"We can go tomorrow."

"Say no more."

"Let's leave early."

"We'll meet at my crib."

"So that means you're doing tha driving?"

"I didn't say all that."

As soon as my phone started to ring I knew it was Paradise from tha ring tone.

"Yo."

"Wow is that how you answer ya phone now?"

"I hope you didn't call to argue."

"Actually, I called to see how you were doing since I haven't heard from you since you got some pussy."

"I been busy I do own three biz-nesses."

"They said you would say that."

"Oh, did they?"

"What tha shot wasn't good enough for you?"

"You crazy."

"Yeah you'd like me to think that."

"Anyway, are you going to that Diva's and Bosses party Saturday night?"

"I don't know."

"Amir please, you know damn well you going."

"No I don't, my boys are trying to talk me into it as we speak."

"You might be able to buck up on something."

"I don't want or need no gold digger. Most of them chicks is looking for a sponsor and I'm not tha one."

"He's going!" Stylz yelled into my phone.

"Me, Mayla, and Roxy are going to New York Friday to get something to wear."

"They wanna go tomorrow."

"Why don't we all go together?"

"We'll have to rent a bus to do that."

"Not if we just follow y'all."

"Well..."

"Oh never mind, I forgot I have to be in court that's why we going Friday."

"You sure?" I asked.

"Yeah, besides I don't want you to see what I get until it's on my body."

"Oh, and what a lovely one you have," I said stroking her ego.

"Amir you something else, I swear you are."

"I didn't say nothing wrong."

"Sometimes it's not what you say but tha way you say it."

"I guess."

"Are you going to be busy later?"

"Depends."

"On?"

"How later you talkin' cause I got an appointment at 7 o'clock that I can't miss."

"I was thinking more on tha lines of 10 o'clock."

"Wait a minute, are you asking for a booty call?"

"If that's what you wanna call it."

"Ha! Ha! Ha! I'd never thought you'd be tha one to call."

"I have needs too."

"When you get something good I guess ain't no shame in ya game when it comes to something you need."

"Nigga pleeeeease, don't start feelin' ya selfya self."

"Trust me Paradise, you're not tha first and you probably won't be tha last."

"Let me find out you one of those hit it and quit it brothers."

"Nah, I'll keep on hitting it until she fucks up then I'll quit it."

"Hopefully, I can stick around."

"That's up to you."

"Well, let me get back to work I'll hit you later."

"A'ight."

"How is tha case going Agent Sharp?"

"Chief, I'm starting to make progress, but I may need more time."

"Agent Sharp I have people that I answer to also, so I need to show them why this is not a waste of time or money."

"Sir, all I can say is this will be worth tha time as well as money."

"I believe you, but my superiors want more than just talk."

"Is there any way I can talk to them?"

"I doubt if it does any good, but you can try."

Once he put tha call through I tried my hand wit tha captain and after much convincing I got them to give me an extension to bring Amir down.

"Agent Sharp."

"Yes Captain."

"Don't let us down, do what ever you need to do to bring him down."

"Yes Sir."


"I was starting to think you weren't going to call."

"My bag I just got tied up."

"Come pick me up."

"Where are you at?"

"Over Mayla's."

"Give me 20 minutes."

"Just call when you close, and I'll come out."


"Look at you all giddy."

"Bitch don't be mad."

"Never would, I be mad when Tex will be here shortly."

"Paradise, do you remember a few months ago when she was frontin' like she didn't like Tex?"

"Sure do, look at her now open like a 24-hour gas station. To hear her tell it he's her man. Question is are you his woman?"

"Roxy you always hatin'."

"Not hatin' just keeping it real."

"Ever since you and Stylz made it official you've been on some bullshit wit me and Tex's relationship."

"I actually call it looking out for my friend."

"Well, if you know something just tell me."

"I always do..." (BEEP-BEEP) "that's my ride bye Bitches."

"Don't suck too hard."

"Ha! Ha! Ha! I'll try not to!" I said licking my lips.

"Took you long enough."

"I had to make a few stops. Any particular hotel you wanna go to?"

"Why can't we just go to your house?"

"Because I don't let people know where I live, you never know who might be trying to line you up to get robbed."

"Damn, that's how you think of me? Never mind don't even answer that. Amir you got trust issues, not that I blame you in your line of work. What motel you going to?"

"My house."

"Don't go there on my account."

"I'm just trying to save you some money."

"Save me some money?"

"Yeah, tonight was on you."

"Really."

"You ask for tha date, so you pay."

"It's not a problem." When I pulled up to my house I had to punch in tha security code.

"I don't think you have to worry about anybody robbing you."

"If there's one thing I know is if tha wolves want you they'll get you, it comes wit tha game."

"Yup sure does."

"This is a big ass house, my pop pop left it to me."

"Ya pop pop must have been a real wealthy guy."

"Very wealthy."

"How did you get mixed up in tha game."

"I was already in tha game tha money he left me just helped out."

"You told me you used that money to start your biz-nesses."

"I did."

"And you also funded this multi-million-dollar drug biz-ness of yours."

*"Damn this bitch should've been a fisherman tha way she always fishing."*

"Am I right?"

"No."

"So how did... Would you like a drink?" I asked cutting her off.

"Do you have some Remy?"

"I have what ever you want."

"Hmm, I'm sure you do. Where's tha bathroom? I want to get comfortable."

"Up tha stairs to tha right."

# CHAPTER 9

## Them Lil Niggaz Ain't Playin' No Games

"Look what you get when you be good."

I looked up from tha blunt I was rolling to see Spinx coming up tha block. Since we were now getting a lot of paper could've easily paid somebody to kill him, but I'd rather put my own work in.

"You ready Buck?"

"Hold on Twist slow down," Twist was still reckless, but I always kept him under control, "no need to draw any attention to ourselves."

"You're right, so what you want to do?"

"Wait on him." We waited close to two hours before Spinks decided to leave.

"About Fuckin' time."

"Damn Twist you need to have patience."

"I know."

"Wit all this money we makin' now you definitely have to have patience."

"I'm trying Buck, I'm trying."

"Niggaz fear us so we don't have to be on our bullshit, especially since we got paper now. Don't get to close I don't want him to spot us."

"Chill out Nigga, I got this we've done this a million times."

"Fuck!"

"What's tha matter?"

"He's headed to Joe's."

"Well, we need to hit him before he goes in."

"Nah, we gon' wait, I don't wanna make Joe's spot hot." I could tell

Twist wasn't happy about it, but he didn't say anything.

"Don't be surprised if we're here all night."

"You got something to do?"

"Nope."

"Well relax and roll this up." We smoked blunt after blunt before we realized we had been sitting there for four hours.

"Yo Buck this nigga ain't coming out no time soon."

"Just be patient, he'll be out soon."

10 minutes later, Spinx came out wit out a care in tha world.

"I bet he's going to tha Bath House."

"Where ever he's going it will be his last stop ever." Sure enough, Spinks pulled up to tha Bath House.

"Let's let him get comfortable before we go in. Here put this on." I hate to admit Fourty definitely was schooling Buck.

POP! POP! POP! POP! POP! POP! POP! POP!

"Oh Shit!"

We both ducked down inside tha car until we no longer heard any shots. When we looked up Spinx was laid out on tha payment.

"Looks like somebody beat us to tha punch."

"They sure did, let's get outta here before tha cops come."

"Now that we don't have to worry about them Niggaz no more we can really get it this paper."

"I'm definitely feeling you on that Buck."

When we got back to tha block it was jumping like fireworks on tha 4th of July.

"Damn, I was just about to hit you niggaz. Is everything straight?"

"Nah, we just about done wit that work."

"Say word."

"Word."

"A'ight give me 30 minutes."

"I know how you get long winded, so hurry up."

"When it comes to that paper I'll be right back."

"Buck do we have enough to hold us down til we holla at Fourty?"

"Yeah but Imma hit my uncle while I'm going to get tha rest of tha work."

"Aye Buck."

"Yo."

"Spend everything."

"If something happens we won't have funds to re-up."

"That's a chance we have to take."

"Fuck it, we came in wit nothing."

"How much doe we holding on to?"

"$420,000."

"That'll get us 21."

"Nigga after we flip we'll officially be millionaires."

"I know, I know, that my shit got hard just thinking about it."

"Nigga you stupid as Hell."

"You need me to go wit you?"

"Nah I'm good, just hold tha block down til I get back."


"Yo Stylz them little niggaz ain't playing no games."

"What you talkin Fourty?"

"My nephew and Twist just called to re-up."

"They ran through all 6 of them already?"

"Yup and now they want 21."

"Yeah right."

"Seriously."

"DAAAMMN, they on a mission for real."

"I'm glad to see them get that paper instead of shooting up tha whole city."

"Now wit them two little niggaz out here getting money it can mean trouble."

"I doubt it, I've been schooling my nephew as of late on how to handle certain situations wit out wildin' out. That's probably why we haven't heard nothing about them."

"When are you going to let them know that we know it's them and not this Strap dude?"

"I'm in no rush."

"Imma ride wit you."

"Cool come on."

"So, what's up wit you and Roxy?"

"Nothing, we decided to try it out see where it goes."

"In other words, she's wifey now?"

"If that's what you want to call her."

"Nigga who you think you fooling, out of all of us you're tha only one who was ever a one-woman man."

"I just choose not to be a player."

"Don't get me wrong, ain't nothing wrong wit it if that's what you choose to do."

"Can we talk about something else besides my love life?"

"Sure, who do you think will win tha Super Bowl this year?"

"As much as I hate to say it, those Packers are looking good again."

"Don't let Amir hear you say that."

"I bleed Eagle Green Fuck tha Packers! How you gon' be from Philly rooting for another squad?"

"Man, you know Amir, fly to Wisconsin every Green Bay home game."

"I would too if I was a season ticket holder."

"You are."

"Yeah but I only have to go to tha Linc."

"One thing I can say is you two niggaz are die-hard fans for real."

"What can I say, I love my Eagles."


"What you two niggaz talkin' bout?"

"My Eagles."

"Awe Nigga y'all ain't makin' no noise tha road to tha Super Bowl has to go through Green Bay and I got one question. Who gon' stop us?"

"My Eagles."

"Nigga y'all might not even make tha playoffs at tha rate y'all going."

"Oh, we gonna be in tha playoffs, you better hope we don't play y'all."

"If y'all do, it's gonna be tha same results as last year."

"Nah, I doubt that."

"I don't, we playing like tha Super Bowl champs, we are."

"Y'all not winning no more Super Bowls."

"Put a stack on it."

"A stack?"

"Yeah, a stack Nigga."

"Nah, bet five stacks."

"It's a bet, I was trying to save you some money."

"I saw Buck earlier today."

"I'm bout to go holla at him now, them little niggaz finally getting at this paper. Man, they want 21."

"21?"

"Yeah, they got that block doing major numbers."

"I see."

"Amir I'm proud of them, they ain't on that wilding out shit no more."

"Money will make anybody calm down, you should know that."

"So, what's tha deal wit Paradise?"

"Nothing."

"I saw ya old mom tha other day."

"Oh yeah?"

"Yeah, Amir I'm not gon' hold you, she bad as a Mafucka and she only look about 30."

"I'm on my way to tha mall to grab her something from Vicky's."

"Wow it's official, she got you."

"She know how to treat a nigga."

"Huh, I bet she do."

"Well, let me go holla at Buck."

"A'ight be safe." I ended up running into Paradise, Roxy, and Mayla at tha mall.

"Well, Well, Well, if it isn't Mister Amir himself."

"What's that suppose to mean Mayla?"

"Nothing, nothing at all."

"So what brings you to tha mall?" Paradise asked looking at tha Victoria Secret bag in my hand.

"I had to pick up something for a friend."

"Must be a really special friend," I didn't answer I just shrug my shoulders, "well don't let us hold you up playa." All I could do was smile and walk away.

"Bitch you crazy."

"Ain't she putting him on tha spot."

"It probably was for you."

"He would have said that."

"Not if it was gon' be a surprise."

"That shit was not for me."

"How are you so sure?"

"Because I just am."

Not that I had too but I choose to stop and grab Paradise something from Vicky's too. My phone alerted me that I had an incoming text. I read tha text that said, **"I hope you enjoy yourself tonight wit that special friend!"**

*I hope I do too,* I thought as I smiled.

I had a special night planned for me and Liz and couldn't wait. When I got there all tha lights were out which meant Liz was still at tha spa. I looked at my watch, 7 o'clock good I have just enough time to do what I need to do.

# CHAPTER 10

## Amir Leaves Romantic Notes for Liz

"Oh Shit! I let time get away from me I need to go home and start dinner."

"Whew, he hasn't gotton here yet."

"When I got to tha door there was a note on it addressed to me."

> Please follow all
> instructions given.
> Once inside take all
> your clothes off and
> head to tha bathroom

A big smile came across my face as I did what I was told. I was expecting to see Amir when I got into tha bathroom but instead there was another note taped to tha mirror.

> Hey there Beautiful
> I took tha pleasure of
> drawing you a nice milk
> bath so please enjoy after
> you're finish head to tha
> bedroom

*"Wow, how did he know I love milk baths?"* It felt so good I dozed off for a few minutes.

"Let me get my ass outta here."

Once I dried off I headed to tha bedroom where there was a Victoria Secrets box wit another letter attached to it.

> Hey Beautiful
>
> It's me again put this on
>
> then come downstairs

"MMM, MMM, MMM that boy got some good taste," I said pulling out tha peach teddy wit matching panties, "how good is this going to look on me."

I had tha perfect pair of Chanel pumps to go wit it. I casually made my way downstairs where there was a candle lit table wit my favorite meal on it.

"Now who did he get to cook this? Oh My God, whoever cooked this ain't no joke in tha kitchen."

"Thank you," Amir said startling me.

"My bag didn't mean to scare you."

"You did not cook this."

"I don't know why I didn't."

"I didn't know you could cook."

"That's because you always got dinner already done when I get here."

"Well, you ain't got to worry about that no more."

This was a onetime thing."

"Oh really?"

"Yup."

"What's tha occasion?"

"Didn't know it had to be one."

"You better be careful somebody might think you were catching feelings."

"Liz you do so much for me I just figured why not do something nice for you."

"Amir, I need to be totally honest wit you."

"It's tha only way to be."

"I love you and I know that we said we would just sit back and enjoy tha ride, but I can't help tha way I feel. I know you don't feel tha same way I do and it's a'ight, I don't expect you to say you love me."

"Liz, let me just say..."

"No hold on let me finish. Amir, we've been dealing wit each other for almost a year so of course my feelings are involved now. Shit, if you remember a few months back I told you I was catching feelings for you. I also know you don't feel tha same way and you want to keep doing you."

"Can I talk now?"

"Sure."

"Liz you're right, I do want to keep doing me but at tha same time I'm not going to front or lie I do have feelings for you. Is it love? Honestly, I don't know but it's something." He just made my night and doesn't even know it.

"Liz, if I can't be wit you and nobody else then I would not put you through tha bullshit."

"I respect that because you didn't have to say that, you could've just went wit it and still did you."

"I respect you too much to do that."

Amir I'm cool wit having an open relationship."

"Why would you want to?"

"Simply because I know that eventually you'll get tired, not to mention none of them will have shit on me." I didn't respond I just swooped her up and headed straight to tha bedroom for a night of unforgettable sex.


Tha next morning, I awoke to tha smell of blueberry waffles, scrambled eggs, home fries, and beef scrapple.

"Good morning Sleepyhead."

"Good morning, what time is it?"

"10 o'clock."

"Shit I overslept, why didn't you wake me?"

"Because you looked cozy plus I knew you needed tha rest."

"How thoughtful of you, next time please wake me up."

"You have some place you need to be?"

"No, I just don't like sleeping in late."

"Boy this ain't late."

"To me it is."

"Are you going to eat or be mad that I didn't wake you sooner?"

"I'm not mad."

"Good, cause if you were I wasn't giving you any of this," I said opening my robe exposing my nude body.

"Even if I was, how could I be after seeing this?" I asked rubbing my hand across her pussy cat.

"Eat ya breakfast before it gets cold."

"That's not all I want to eat."

We ended up staying in bed all night only getting out to shower and eat.

"UNH, UNH, UNH, and you wonder why a bitch all in love."

"So, do you have any plans for your birthday next week?"

"Me and Joanne are going to dinner."

"That's it?"

"Yeah, that's enough for me."

"Oh that's right, you don't need all that over-the-top stuff as you call it."

"Amir, even though I may look like it I'm not no young girl, it doesn't take much to make or keep me happy. As long as I can have a few orgasms a week I'm good."

"I bet you are."

"And as long as you strap up."

"You're tha only one I ride bareback."

"I better be."

"Trust me you are."

"I bet you say that to all tha girls," Liz said playfully pushing me.

We had another round of wow but passionate sex then afterword's we jumped in tha shower.

"Damn, how did I let this young boy put it on me like that."

*"I've had a lot of sex in my 20 years of living but none as good as Liz,"* I thought to myself as I washed her back and ass. I could feel her making her ass bounce as I was washing it.

"You bout to start something."

"Nothing I can't finish."

And just like that it was on once again.


"I might need to buy some boxes to keep over here."

"Look in tha top drawer."

"Wow."

"Well, I figured when you take a shower you would want to change your boxers."

"See that's why I fuck wit you, you always be thinking about a nigga."

"Maybe too much."

"Is that such a bad thing?"

"Nah, not at all."

"I've got some things to take care of, I'll see you later."

"A'ight be safe."

"I will."

"Amir."

"Yo."

"I love you."

"That's what's up," I said not quite sure how to respond even though I did feel tha same way, but I refuse to let her know.

# CHAPTER 11

## Agent Sharp Who's in tha Photo

"Who are these people in this photo Agent Sharp?"

"Tha one in red is Fourty, tha one in black is Stylz, tha one in blue this Tex, and you already know that's Amir."

"I'm not 100% percent sure, but I think he gets his shipment on Wednesdays. I'm hoping to get some pictures of them wit tha work."

"How do you plan on doing that?"

"I don't know but I'll figure something out."

"Agent Sharp don't compromise ya selfya self or your job."

"Chief trust me, there's nothing I want more than to see Amir behind bars rotting in jail for tha rest of his life."

"So, do I but you need to be safe Agent Sharp."

"I have it all under control Chief."

"A'ight, if you need anything you be sure to let me know."

"Since you mentioned it, I could use a few of those micro cameras."

"Make me a list of everything you need, and I'll have it first thing in tha morning."

"OK thank you Chief." As I left tha building I couldn't help but smile at tha thought of bringing Amir down.


"Yo Buck ain't that Home Girl coming out tha Federal building?"

"Who?"

"Home Girl?"

"Nigga I don't know you talkin' bout."

"Never mind, I'm probably trippin'. Sasha told me to let you know she wants to holla at you."

"Oh, now she see a nigga getting at a dollar she wanna give a nigga some rhythm."

"You know how they do."

"I sure do and I'm good, Fuck her!"

"That's what I would do."

"Nah, I'm not going to give her tha satisfaction. Speak of tha devil," I said seeing Sasha as we pulled up to McDonalds on Broad.


"Hey Buck."

"What up Sash?"

"Hey Twist."

"Sash."

"Did you tell him?"

"Tell me what?" I asked acting like I didn't know what she talking about.

"I told Twist to tell you I wanted to holla."

"Listen Sash, you wasn't trying to get at me before I was getting this paper."

"I know and that's because you was buck wild."

"I still am."

"No you're not, you've calmed down a lot besides I could care less about ya money."

"That's what ya mouth say."

"And its tha truth Sweety."

"It's only one way to find out," Twist said before either of us could say anything.

"Mind ya biz-ness."

"Now it's mind my biz-ness, you was not saying that when you wanted me to tell him you was trying to holla."

"Thank you but I got it from here."

"I'll order ya food while you talk to Sash."

"Just get me a Number 3 wit a Strawberry milkshake."


"So what's up Buck?"

"This paper, that's what's up."

"Nigga I'm talkin' bout wit me."

"I don't know, what's up wit you?"

"So, you do have a sense of humor."

"Sorry but I wasn't being funny," I said in a serious tone.

"No need to get all serious I was only jokin'."

"Yeah, so was I."

"Are you going to take my number?"

"No, but you're more than welcome to have mine."

"Can you at least put it in my phone?"

"I can do that." Once I put my number in her I-phone she asked if she could take my picture.

"Fuck you trying to line me up?"

"Boy no, I just want to put it wit ya numbers, so it will show up when ever I call, or you decided to call me."

"In that case, go ahead." Twist came out while she was talking my picture.

"Fuck was that about?"

"Do you ever mind ya biz-ness Twist?"

"Not when it comes to my boy his biz-ness is my biz-ness."

"Not this time."

"He'll tell me."

Sash looked at me then said, "Damn that's how you get down?"

"Nah, he just messing wit you."

"A'ight I gotta go, I'll call you later."

"You do that."

I watched as Sash walked away ass bouncing like crazy.

"UNH, UNH, UNH."

"What?"

"She fat to death."

"You ain't gotta tell me."

"I know you gonna hit that."

"Damn right and I'll tell you all about it."

"Damn they always puttin' all this mafuckin salt on their fries."

"Take 'em back."

"I'm not going through all that."

"Then stop complaining, you always do that."

"Did Jake pay you that doe yet?"

"Yeah, he hit me this morning."

"I'm bout to holla at Fourty."

"I think we should just grab 25 from now on."

"We can do that since we dumping that every three weeks anyway."

"A'ight let me make tha call."

"Buck see if you can get us some of that good green they got."

"To smoke?"

"Yeah and to put on tha block since people always askin' for it."

"Damn, I never even thought about that."

"Nigga we might as well get all this money, ain't no need playing wit it."

"Fo' sure."

"Well, I'll hit you on tha way back."

"You want me to send Shanky wit you?"

"Nah, I'm good Imma take tha Honda."

"Oh yeah, I keep forgetting Fourty hooked us up wit those stash boxes."

"Dog, proof it don't get no better than that."

"Who you telling."

"Before you leave go holla at Mrs. Dee, she needed to see you."

"I was on my way to holla at her anyway."

"Nigga you hittin' that?"

"Shit I wish I was, she fatter than a Mafucka."


"Mrs. Dee, Twist said you wanted to holla at me."

"Yeah I did."

"You did, or you do?"

"I do. I respect tha way you take care of ery body on tha block."

"It's tha least I can do, wit out y'all me and Twist wouldn't be able to do what we do."

"Imma be up front, I could use some extra money and I hear that you could use another place for your stuff."

"Actually, I do."

"Well, I'll be willing to help you out if tha price is right."

"I'm willing to give you a stack a week."

"A stack?"

"You don't think that's enough?"

"Hell yeah, I'm just surprised you'd be willing to give that much up."

"Why not, you're doing me a huge favor, so I have no problem showing how much I appreciate it."

"Say no more."

"I'm on my way to grab some shit now so I'll be back in a minute."

"Here take this key and get a copy."

"I'll bring tha money back when I come back."

"What's up Nephew?"

"I need 25 and what's tha number on some of that good green y'all got?"

"Personal or sell?"

"Both."

"850 a pound."

"Let me get 10 of 'em."

"A'ight, same place 30 minutes."

When I pulled up Fourty was already there.

"How long you been here Unc?"

"I just pulled up right before you. Make sure you call ya mom she's worried about you."

"I actually sent her some flowers and was taking her to dinner."

"That's good cause I told her I hit you wit a nice piece of money, so you wouldn't have to be in tha streets."

"Good lookin' Unc."

"Buck, I don't like lying to ya mom so at some point you gon' need to come clean wit her."

"I know but not right yet."

"A'ight but just make sure you do it."

"Damn Unc, I know you not scared of big sis?"

"Nah but we don't lie to each other either."

"I respect that and I'm sorry for putting you in this position."

"When I do tell her, I won't say you knew, she'll probably tell me to deal wit you anyway."

"You're probably right."

"Come on you know my mom's."

"Yup sure do and if she doesn't find out from you we'll both be in for it."

"Just give me two weeks."

"Oh yeah Unc, I need one more of these cars for Tweet."

"No problem give me a few days. Buck, I didn't want for you. I do what I do so you would not have to."

"Unc I know but it was time for me to get my own bread and not depend on you."

"I understand, and I am proud of you for being ya own man standing on ya own two feet."

"I just took ya advice about thinking before reacting."

"That explains why tha body count is down in tha city."

"Come on Unc, that wasn't all me."

"I know, you and Twist," he said wit a smile, "I'm just glad you're on my side."

"Well, you can rest assure I'm on this paper chase right now unless a Mafucka cross me."

"Hopefully that will not happen, if it does call me I got people to handle that."

"No doubt, I'll hit you up Unc."

"Cool be safe."

# CHAPTER 12

## We Party Like Rock Stars

"I know this party is going to be off tha hook," Roxy said while putting on her Pierre Hardy pumps.

"Well, I don't think Tex and his boys have yet to disappoint wit one of their parties."

"Why is tha theme called ladies and gentlemen?"

"Because ladies wear dresses and gentlemen wear suits."

"True, true!" Mayla yelled while dapping me.

"Well, there will be no question as to which ladies will be tha flyest."

"Is there ever?"

"Unfortunately not."

"Paradise are you and Amir still playing games or did y'all make it official yet?"

"Girl I'm starting to think he already got a main chick."

"Why you say that?"

"It just seems like it."

"Why not just ask him."

"Like he gonna tell tha truth."

"Yeah you probably right."

"It still won't hurt to ask."

"Shit I wouldn't care, looks to me like you're tha one getting all tha time."

"Yeah but I'm also tha one waking up to an empty bed so at tha end of tha day who's really tha fool?"

"Y'all crazy, I would love to just be able to call up somebody when I just want a wet ass and not have to deal wit tha bullshit that goes wit tha relationship."

"Bitch stop lying, you love Stylz."

"You're right I do but if I could go back and just be fuck buddies I would."

"Uh Oh, sounds like trouble in paradise."

"No not at all, I just wouldn't mind doing me sometimes."

"I hear that."

"Come on so we can make our grand entrance."


"You niggaz always fly."

"We're tha host we gotta be."

"You two little niggaz lookin' like new money."

"We just tryin' to keep up wit y'all."

"Y'all doing a pretty good job at it."

"Buck you know ya mom gon' be there tonight."

"I know we went shoppin' together."

"She called me tha other day and let me know you was pumpin'."

"I told her you didn't know and not to tell you."

"Of course, she told me, she was going to let you know and that I should holla at you if I was going to be in tha game."

"I know she told me she didn't want you involved in tha game but since you were for me to deal wit you. See Unc it all worked out."

"Lucky for us. I was thinking about getting that 750 ya mom wants for her birthday next month."

"We can go half on it. Or I can just put tha rims and system on it."

"We can go half on everything."

"Works for me. Speaking of my mom I have to pick her up in 15 minutes."

"You better go you know how she is when you're not on time."

"A'ight I'll see you later."

When me and Twist pulled up my mom was coming out tha house."

"How did you know we were pulling up?"

"Are you kidding, how could I not know wit that loud ass music?"

"I told him to turn it down Ms. Classy."

"Boy hush ya mouth, I know damn well you didn't tell him to turn it down."

"Nah he didn't Ma."

"Damn Nigga when we start doing that?"

"Watch ya mouth," my mom said smacking Twist in tha back of his head.

"AAAAH Ms. Classy."

"Ah my ass."

"Listen to you cursing Mom."

"And I'm grown too. Have to talk to ya uncle today?"

"I just left him before I picked you up."

"What he talking about?"

"Nothing just that you told him I was on my grind."

"Of course I did, he's ya uncle who just happens to be winning."

"I told him I was going to holla at him on my next flip."

"You make sure you do that."

"Mom I got this."

"I don't want you selling drugs but if you are, you need to be in it to win it not just to show off."

"That goes wit out saying."

"I hope you don't plan on making a career out of it either."

"Nah Mom, I'm just trying to get in and out wit no problems."

"I hope so cause ya uncle said tha same thing and look at him, successful and still in it."

We pulled up into V.I.P. behind my uncle's car.

"You just now getting here?"

"Yeah, I had some biz-ness to take care of. Look at you Sis looking like a young girl."

"Nah, I just take care of myself."

"Imma have to keep my eye on you tonight."

"No you don't, we got that covered," Twist quickly said.

"Y'all better not act a fool tonight."

"Don't give us a reason to."

"Nephew let me school you to something real quick, every time ya mom decides to come out niggaz be all over her, I don't blame them if she wasn't my mom I'd be on her fine ass too."

"AAAH Ma."

"Didn't I just tell y'all about them mouths?"

"My bag. What up Classy?"

"Hey Amir."

"Buck, Twist."

"What up Big Homey?"

"You little niggaz lookin' like money."

"We just trying to earn our spot."

"Looks like y'all already have."

"Not yet but you'll know when we have."

"I heard that, Classy what you drinking tonight?"

"What ever, your money can't afford."

"Fourty you didn't tell me Classy was into comedy now."

"Ha! Ha! Ha! Boy you tha comedian."

"Y'all both funny."

"Nah, just get me my usual."

"Long Island wit a twist of Remy coming right up."


"Come on, Tex told me that they have our names at tha door."

"Good, cause I did not want to stand in this long ass line."

"Me either."

"Roxy, Mayla, and Paradise." Tha bouncer put our arm bands on then let us through tha rope.

"Y'all enjoy yaselves."

"We plan to," Roxy said while walking past.

As soon as we hit tha club tha sounds of Major P's Trouble hit us like a hard punch.

"This is my shit right here," Paradise said shaking her ass like a stripper.

"UNH, UNH, UNH, I see somebody trying to get Fucked tonight."

"Trying? Bitch please, before tha night is over my sweet juices will be all over somebody's shit."

"Somebody or Amir?"

"Depends what I'm in tha mood for."

"Mayla and Paradise you two bitches is Full of Shit."

"Just because Stylz got that butt on lock don't hate on us."

"That's where you wrong, we got each other on lock," Stylz said walking up kissing Roxy on her cheek.

"That's right Boo let 'em know."

"UMM excuse me."

"Amir, Tex and Fourty in V.I.P. What they sent you down here to get us?"

"Don't flatter ya selfya self I seen Roxy, so I decided to come down and make sure she straight."

"I am now."

"Oh My God, will you two give it a rest."

"Ignore them Boo they just mad."

"I know I can see it all in their face."

"Now don't you flatter ya selfya self Stylz."

"Why should I when you're doing such a good job at it."

"I swear y'all are worse than kids."

"It's all out of love, ain't that right Mayla?"

"Yup sure is."

"Yo are y'all gonna stand there and run y'all mouth all night or party?"

"I don't know about them but I'm going to tha bar."

"Me too, hold up Mayla come on Roxy we going to V.I.P."

"And so are we smart ass."

"Girl you and Stylz act like y'all related."

"That's my boy, he cool as shit."

"That's my boy, he cool as shit."

We got to V.I.P. and all tha ballers were there along wit tha groupie broads.

"Hey there Sexy," Amir said grabbing my hand.

I responded wit, "Hey you."

"You looking good tonight."

"So are you."

"Thank you."

"You're welcome."

"What are you drinking tonight?"

"Same thing I always drink."

"Long Island Iced Tea wit a twist of Remy."

"Wit a shot of Remy on tha side."

"Wow, you must have something planned for tha night."

"That's all up to you," I said while winking.

"Say no more."

"Ya fan club is waiting on you."

"That's my little cousin and her crew I'm letting them hang out for a few."

"Boy you got game wit you."

"What ever you say Ms. Paradise."

"You always get so defensive."

"Nah, you so use to niggaz lying to you when I keep it 100 you always think I'm runnin' game."

"Maybe that's what it is."

"Ain't no maybe in it, you know I'm right."

"Are you going to get my drink or talk my head off?"

"Both, so come on." I can't believe it, I was doing exactly what I said I wouldn't do, catch feelings for Amir.


"Aye yo Buck."

"What up Homey?"

"Ain't that's ya peeps over there?"

"Who my peeps."

"Nigga don't act like you don't know who ya peeps is."

"I don't."

"Sasha."

"Man, she want a Mafucka to sweat her and I ain't doing that."

"Don't look now but here she comes."

"Hey Buck, hey Twist."

"What up Sasha."

"Oh, you not speaking Buck?"

"What up Sash?"

"Damn that's how you feel?"

"I ain't playin' that game you playin'."

"I'm not playin' no game I just wanted to see if you wanted me or just some pussy."

"I'm not pressed, I can get pussy anytime I want it."

"I'm pretty sure you can but it won't be as good as this," she said pointing to her stuff.

"You might be right, but I'll never know," I said while walking off.

"Yo Nigga is you crazy?"

"Nah."

"What was that about Sash?"

"Nothing at all Keesh."

"Did you tell Twist what I said?"

"No."

"Bitch you was too busy hollering at Buck."

"Bitch Buck got my panties soaking wet."

"Wow, you need to stop all that fronting and give him some pussy."

"He already has he just doesn't know it yet."

"Well, you might wanna let it be known or you might miss out," I turned to see tha broad Nana in his face, "come on let's get a drink."

"Hey Buck."

"Heeeey Twist."

"Hey Keesh."

"Hey Ma."

"I didn't know y'all do tha club thing."

"We don't but this is a special party my uncle and his team threw."

"Keesh let me holla at you for a sec."

"What up Twist?"

"I told Sash to get at you for me."

"Are you serious because I told her to holla at you for me."

"Say word."

"Word, I'm not lying."

"Look at her all jealous."

"She keep frontin' she gon' end up missing out."

"I told her that."

"Excuse me Buck, let me borrow ya ear for a sec please."

"What Sash you said what you had to say."

"I did but you walked away before I finished."

"Well finish."

"First, tell ya friend you'll get wit her at a later date."

"Now why would I do that?"

"Because you wit me tonight."

"Oh I am?"

"That's up to you and no I'm not playing no games."

"A'ight say no more." Little did she know I wasn't even gon' knock her off tonight.

"Sash that's crazy you ain't tell Keesh what I said."

"My bag, she told me to tell you something too."

"I know she told me."

"Damn Buck, what you forgot I was over here waiting on you?"

"Nah, Imma hit ya phone later."

"Don't be playing."

"I got you Nana."

"Oh, so you got her huh?"

"Imma man of my word so I'll call her and let her know I'll be busy."

"You sure will be busy."

"Sash you something else."

"Why you say that?"

"All of a sudden you want to give me some pussy."

"Boy please, I been wanted to give you some."

"So, you was just frontin then?"

"I guess you can say that, I call it playing hardball."

"Buck who is this?"

*"Damn he got all types of broads on him,"* I thought to myself.

"Sasha this is Classy."

"Oh, now I'm Classy."

"How you doing Sweetie?"

"I'm OK and you?"

"I'm fine but don't worry I'm Buck's mom." Tha look on my face must of said it all.

"I know, I know I don't look old."

"Mom don't start embarrassing me."

"Boy who you think you talkin' to?"

"I'll be back I'm gon' holla at Unc."

"A'ight I'll keep ya girlfriend company."

"She's not my girl Mom."

"We just friends Ms. Classy."

"Please don't call me Ms., just Classy."

"I'm sorry."

"No need to apologize, you're pretty."

"Thank you."

"Look at him telling his uncle on me."

"Now I see where he gets his good looks from."

"I like you already."

"Hopefully I'll be around long enough for us to get to know one another."

"Trust me you will; I know my son and he has tha look in his eyes when he looks at you."


"Yo Nephew she bad as Hell."

"Yeah she is."

"I see ya mom ain't waste no time grilling her."

"You know how she do."

"Do I man, I get it tha same way she's just being concerned."

"I'm cool wit it because she will let me know if she's real or fake."

"That's one thing you don't have to worry about."

"Imma need you first thing in tha morning."

"A'ight, I'll hit you when I get up."

"Nah, Imma hit you cause you probably still be asleep."

"Little Nigga I'm up before tha sun rises every morn no matter what time I go to sleep."

"That makes two of us."

"Looks like you might have ya hands full tonight."

"I'm not hittin' her tonight."

"You not hittin that, Nigga you must of bump ya head."

"Come on Unc you taught me that."

"So you were paying attention?"

"I'm always paying attention even when you might think I'm not."

"I see, I see, I gotta hand it to you Nephew, ever since you been gettin' at this money you really calmed down."

"Unc I need to be honest, me and Twist runnin' tha show."

"I know."

"You know?"

"Buck ain't too much is this town that I don't know about and if I don't, my squad does."

"Why didn't you say anything?"

"I didn't need to as long as you were straight, that was all that really mattered."

"I had to tell you because I didn't like lying to you."

"Trust me I understand, and I know I always got ya back no matter what."

"Thanks that means a lot."


"What are you two over here talkin' about?"

"You don't need to know everything Classy."

"When it comes to my son and brother I do."

"Well since you must know, Buck wanted my opinion on Shorty right here," he said pointing to Sash.

"How bout I give you mines?"

"This ought to be good."

From a brief conversation wit her I think she's smart, confident, and very pretty."

"So, in other words, you like her."

"She reminds me of myself when I was her age."

"Uh oh Nephew you in serious trouble."

"Fourty shut up."

"Nah, I know where this is headed."

"Fill me in Unc."

"Ya mom probably invited her over for dinner so she can really get to know her."

"Mom tell me you didn't."

"Yes, I did invite her to dinner Tuesday night."

"Sash you could've said no."

"Why would I do that ya mom is down to earth."

"Well, y'all have fun."

"Boy you better be there."

"I got biz-ness to handle Tuesday night."

"Well, I suggest you reschedule it then."

"Mom!"

"Mom My Ass, you heard what I said."

"I need a drink, come on Sash."


"Classy why you put him on tha spot like that?"

"He'll be a'ight, jus like you use to."

"Of course, he will that goes wit out saying."

"What up y'all?"

"Nothing Amir."

"Buck said you over here buggin'!"

"Ain't nobody buggin', I'm just being a mom that's all."

"We all know what that's like huh Fourty."

"We sure do."

For tha rest of tha night we partied like rock stars.

# CHAPTER 13

## Agent Sharp Getting Close?

"Please tell me you have something good Agent Sharp."

"I have a few pictures of his workers putting in some work along wit one of his partners dropping some product off."

"Amir is not in any of these."

"No Sir he's very careful but I'm sure he'll slip up soon."

"I hope so, it's been a year and we're still where we started, nowhere."

"Trust me Captain I'm getting close, it's only a matter of time before I get him."

"I hope you're right because my superiors want results."

"I'm just trying to do everything by tha book, I don't want any loop holes."

"And neither do I Agent Sharp, neither do I."

"I'll report in in another few weeks."

# CHAPTER 14

## Where's My Money!

"Do you got that money you owe or what?"

"I got half of it."

(SMACK)

"It's been two months, how you only got half my money?"

"Tex I'll get tha rest I just need another week."

"Mafucka I gave you two months."

"I tried to call you, but you never answer ya phone."

"Nigga it don't matter you should've held it."

"Tex I say we just shoot him in tha knee caps."

"Come on man I just need a week."

"Hold up didn't you just say a couple days I think you trying to play me."

(SMACK, SMACK)

"Let me get this straight it's only gonna take you a week to get tha 10 stacks you owe me?"

"Yes, maybe less."

"Nah Tex that nigga trying to run."

"I swear I'm not, I would've had ya money, but I had to pay my mother's hospital bill."

"Listen, you got one week to have my money or next time won't be no talkin'."

"I got you Tex."

"And I'll still make sure you good."

"I really do appreciate it."

"A'ight I'll holla at you this time next week."

"Aye yo I know you was just Bullshit'n about still hittin' him wit work."

"Nah, Imma still hit 'em."

"After what he just did?"

"Stylz he ain't do nothing we wouldn't have done."

"Nigga we ain't never messed up no fetti."

"I'm talkin' bout paying ya mom's hospital bills."

"Nigga I know you didn't fall for that."

"He ain't lying I can tell, besides he never fucked up money before so why would he start now?"

"I kind of feel bad you smacked him up."

"You gotta do that, if not, he'll think it's OK to fuck up."

"Right, I feel you."

"Yo from what I hear you and Mayla are becoming quite an item."

"Roxy may need to get her facts straight."

"I don't think it's Roxy that needs to get her facts straight."

"Is that right?"

"Hey I'm just saying."

"Well, I'll check Mayla then."

"You might be giving her tha wrong impression."

"Don't get me wrong she's definitely my peoples I got mad love for her I'm just not in love wit her."

"I don't think she knows that."

"She knows, I told her how I feel."

"Ever since Monae broke ya heart you refuse to let ya guard down."

"I keep telling y'all she didn't break my heart."

"Yeah that's what you been telling ya selfya self for tha past 3 years."

"Stylz you know I would never lie to you."

"I would hope not."

"Listen, I was hurt when Monae took my money and left tha state, but I wasn't heart broken."

"I always wondered why you didn't go to Texas and kick her butt?"

"Because evidently, she needed tha money even though she could've ask, and I probably would've gave it to her, no questions asked."

"All Imma say is don't let Monae ruin your chance for happiness."

"I'm just not ready for relationship."

"And you told Mayla this?"

"Yes, and she was a'ight wit it."

"Tex I gotta be honest she's hoping for more."

"I'm not saying I won't catch feelings like that for her because we can't control our heart, but at this point I'm just not there yet."

"I respect that."

"So does she."

"You better not let nobody else scoop her up."

"I'm not worried about that I already know niggaz is trying to kick tha door down to get at her."

"I don't blame them, she Michael Jackson BAD, hell I was kickin' tha door for six months before I got any rhythm wit her."

"Now look at you playing hardball wit her."

"I'm not playing hardball and I'm just keeping it 100."

"Well, I hope you don't miss out."

"Styles all I can do is keep it real and let it all play out."

"No matter what, you know I'll always have ya back."

"Nigga you been having my back since tha sand box."

"Yeah and vice versa, we all ride out for one another."


"What are you two niggaz talkin' bout?"

"Nothing, just how tight all of us are."

"We need to take a vacation, get away for a week or two."

"Man, Roxy gon' wanna come."

"Bring her."

"What I look like bringing sand to tha beach?"

"We can all bring somebody."

"Yeah, I told Liz we needed to get away."

"Nigga how you gon' take Liz and Mayla along wit Roxy gon' be there?"

"What that means?"

"Paradise."

"She not my girl, I don't owe her no explanation."

"You can take Liz on a trip wit tha two of y'all."

"So, who you gon' take Fourty?"

"I don't know, I'll probably bring Jazzman."

"Damn Nigga you're still knocking her off?"

"Amir they might as well move in together she over his spot so much."

"Let me find out you all caught up."

"Nigga that's my peoples."

"Hey if that's what it is then that's what it is."

"Would I lie to y'all?"

"We hope not."

"You dudes is funny."


## "I BEAT THA PUSSY UP"

"Hello."

"Hey you busy?"

"Nah."

"How about dinner?"

"Sounds good, plus I need to ask you something anyway."

"So ask me."

"I'll wait til dinner."

"Must be serious."

"Not really, what time you picking me up?"

"Picking you up?"

"Oh, so now I don't speak English?"

"Shut up and be ready by 8 o'clock."

"Yes Ma'am."


"Damn Playboy trying to make it all romantic."

"She invited me to dinner, so I figured I just ask her then. By tha way, where do y'all wanna go?"

"Hawaii."

"Y'all sure that's a 10-hour flight."

"None of us has ever been but you."

"Well, Hawaii it is then. I'll get up wit y'all later."

"You know damn well we not gonna see you til tomorrow."

"You're probably right."

"Because if you don't stay wit Paradise you're definitely staying wit Liz."

"I'll get wit y'all tomorrow then."

"Hit me later and let me know if Paradise is going wit you."

"Jus book me for two of tha best suites they have."

"Will do. What day should I book it for?"

"I need to check wit Jazzman to make sure she can get off for a week."

"Oh shit, I need to do tha same wit Roxy."

"Me too."

"Well, I suggest y'all call and find out."

"What about if Paradise can't get off?"

"I'll just take Liz."

"What if she can't get off?"

"She makes her own hours."

"That's right, she has her own biz-ness."

"I'm out, I'll holla at y'all tomorrow."


(BEEP-BEEP) When I walked outside Paradise was sitting in a black on black Audi A-8 wit 22's.

"I know you didn't come pick me up in no niggas car."

"Don't disrespect me Amir this is my shit!"

"Excuse me, I just never seen this before and we been talkin' for a while now."

"I don't drive it too often."

"Yeah I see."

"Are you going to get in or not?"

"You in a rush?"

"I just want to make sure we not late because I made reservations."

"A'ight, let's go then."


"Roxy did Stylz ask you to go to Hawaii wit him for a week?"

"Bitch yes."

"Damn they must of ask all of us to go."

"I know cause my cousin Jazz said Fourty ask her to go too."

"Well, Paradise didn't call and say anything."

"Amir probably ask somebody else after she turned him down."

"Roxy she not turning down no trip to Hawaii."

"I know but it sounded good."

"I know if he doesn't ask her she's gonna be mad."

"Why would she be mad?"

"Because she really likes him."

"Well, I guess we'll see if he feels tha same way.

"We definitely will."

"I don't know but I'll be in Hawaii having a ball."

"Me and you both."


We were waiting for our food when Amir ask me if I could get off work for a week.

"I'm sure I probably could."

"Good, I want you to go to Hawaii wit me."

"Hawaii?"

"Yes, if you don't want to go I'll understand."

"Amir stop playing, I would love to go to Hawaii wit you."

"Roxy and Mayla will be there to keep you company."

"So, you must be going on biz-ness?"

"Nah."

"Then why would I need them to keep me company?"

"I don't know, we all just wanted to take a much-needed vacation and they thought we should bring somebody wit us."

"Oh, so I'm only being asked because they're going?"

"Not at all, I could've ask anybody."

"You probably thought they would tell me."

"Paradise you're not my girl."

"No but we been wit each other for tha past 8 ½ months."

"I don't want to sound ignorant but 8 ½ months ain't Shit!"

"You right," I said wit an attitude.

*"Damn I must of hit a nerve,"* I thought to myself.

"Amir you can take somebody else I won't be tha least bit upset."

I knew she was mad, but I didn't care I was just keeping it real as I always do.

"Paradise if I wanted to take someone else I would've never ask you."

I didn't respond wit anything smart I just said, "Thank you for inviting me."

"You're more than welcome."


After eating Paradise invited me to stay tha night wit her. Even though I wanted to I had already told Liz that I would be over her house tonight.

"I'm not going to be able to stay wit you tonight."

"In other words, you already got some pussy lined up?"

"It never stops wit you does it?"

"Amir you don't have to feed me no bullshit!"

"I never do, now whether or not you believe it that's solely up to you."

"So, you telling me you never lie?"

"Nah."

"A'ight since we being honest, we are being honest right?"

"Aren't we always?"

"So, what so important that you can't stay wit me?" *I thought about lying but I decided to keep it real.*

"I told my peoples I would stay wit her tonight."

"Wow, she really got you open."

"Ha! Ha! Ha!"

"That's funny huh?"

"Yeah."

"Tha truth always is."

"Paradise, I told you about my peoples from day one."

"I'm curious, why didn't you take her to Hawaii?"

"Because I ask you to go that's why."

"I guess I should be honored."

"That's up to you."

"Amir you're a smart ass."

"I'll take that as a compliment coming from you."

Paradise dropped me back off, I went to kiss her and she turned her head causing my kiss to land on her cheek.

"Damn that's how you feel?"

"Call me tomorrow or whenever it's convenient for you."

I got out wit out responding. I told myself I wouldn't let my feelings get involved but here I am acting petty like a young girl. I might need to fall back from Amir because I don't like tha way I'm acting."

# CHAPTER 15

## Tha New Product

"Agent Sharp I talked to my superiors and they're pleased wit your report."

"Chief, I'm getting close."

"I know that's why they decided to give you an additional two years."

"Oh My God, thanks Chief."

"Agent Sharp I should be thanking you, this is tha closest anyone has ever gotten to Amir Adams."

"Wit this extra time I'm sure to bring him down."

"You just take your time and be safe Agent Sharp."

"I will Chief."

# CHAPTER 16

## Hawaii

"Buck is that shawty that be wit ya girl?"

"Who my girl?"

"Nigga you know who I'm talkin' bout."

"I keep telling you I don't have no girl we just friends."

"Well, she didn't get tha memo because according to Keesh y'all a couple."

"My mom keep telling her that bullshit."

"Ms. Classy really likes her."

"Yeah I know, she wifey material."

"True but I'm not ready to be wit just one chick."

"Did you tell her?"

"Twist I told her that a few months ago."

"What's wrong wit having ya cake and eating it too."

"If Imma be wit her then that's all it is. Like you and Keesh," I said smiling.

"I'm not gonna lie that's my baby, she keep it real wit a nigga."

"Hell nah, I know you not going soft on a nigga?"

"Only thing soft about me is my clothes I throw on."

"You know my Unc and his boys going to Hawaii for a week."

"Well, we need to get at him before they roll."

"Already on top of that."

"Did you talk to Scrap?"

"Nah, I haven't seen him."

"He said he had something for you."

"Why didn't you get it from him?"

"I tried but he wanted to give it to you himself."

"I guess he don't trust you."

"Buck tha nigga probably only had a stack on him."

"If he was looking for me, he had 3,500 on him."

"Why didn't he just call you?"

"He doesn't have this number and I left my other phone at tha crib."

"What's tha deal wit Keesh brother?"

"I talk to him and let him know he had to come to tha table wit something. He should be getting back at me no later than tomorrow if he really trying to get at this paper."

"He'll get at you trust me."

"I Always do."

"You got everything you need?"

"Yep."

"You sure?" I asked sarcastically.

"Positive."

"Well let's go, ery body is meeting up at Stylz and Roxy's crib."

"Better make sure you got everything you're always tha one forgetting something."

"Oh Shit."

"What?"

"My iPod."

"See, I told you."

"I need that for tha flight."

"I was kind a hoping we could dip off and make our own turbulence."

"Them bathrooms is little Jazz."

"If you scared then say you scared."

"Like Bone Krusher said I Ain't Neva Scared."

"That's all it is then."

"Jazz you a bonafide freak."

"Only for you."

"I hear you."

"Fourty don't try to play me."

"All I said was I hear you."

"It was tha way you said it."

"Don't take it personal Baby girl."

"You know how tight this pussy was when you got it so stop playing."

Jazz was right, that thing was like virgin pussy when I first hit it.

"Well now it's molded to fit me."

"Ha! Ha! Ha! Boy you so stupid."

"So, what are we doing?"

"Going to Hawaii."

"I'm talkin' about us."

"What do you mean?"

"Where is this going or is it going anywhere?"

"That's funny, I was wondering tha same thing."

"Come on we can talk on our way."

As soon as we got in tha car she said, "It has been a year."

"I know, I thought you was cool wit how things were."

"Fourty, I never express my feelings cause I didn't want to scare you off."

"Well, you can express them now."

"I love you and I have been for tha last few months."

"Jazz I'm going to be completely honest, I don't know if this is love I feel for you, but I know I feel something."

"I figured that much out when you stop having drugs in my house."

"At first, I thought it was because you were always over here but then I came to tha conclusion that you cared about me a little."

"Jazz you know you my baby and when I feel love I promise you'll be tha first to know."

"Awe how considerate of you." When we got to Roxy's and Stylz's ery body was already there.

"Y'all was about to be left."

"You said be here by 9 o'clock."

"What time is it now?"

I looked at my watch, "Damn my bag."

I grabbed our luggage then headed to tha van Tex had rented so we wouldn't all have to drive to tha airport.


By tha time our plane landed it was 6 o'clock. We were met by some of tha most beautiful women I have ever seen in my life.

"Do all tha women look like this?"

"Man, I'm quite sure they got plenty of ducks to go along wit all this beauty."

"Shit, Mayla better act right or I'll be bringing one of these bad ass bitches back to tha states wit me."

"I heard that Playa."

"He gonna get himself and her killed."

"I might not take me one back but Imma surely hit me some Hawaiian pussy before I leave."

"I am definitely wit you on that," Amir said wit a devilish smile.

"How are we going to pull that off Fourty ask?"

"You know my man Katul is from here and he just happens to be here visiting his parents."

"So that's why we here?"

"You're tha ones who chose Hawaii, not me."

"You were right we did."

"All I did was call Katul to find out what spots was jumping, and he informed me that he would be here visiting."

"So it all worked out."


"What are y'all over here plotting on?"

"Trying to figure out where to get some of that good weed from."

"I should've known."

"We gonna be here for a week I need me some good green."

"How about we get to tha hotel and check in first?" I could Mayla wanted to get her thing off she was still roused up from this morning.

"That's our ride right there."

"I need me a drink."

"Bitch you had enough on tha plane."

"Those water down drinks, they robbing people wit out no gun."

"We might need to check Roxy into AA!"

"Bitch please, I don't need no fucking AAA!" We all started laughing.

When we arrived at our hotel there were at least four bellhops standing out front.

"Ooh he's cute," Paradise said referring to tha one who grabbed our luggage.

I didn't say anything because truth be told I didn't care. Even though I've been seeing Paradise for 8 ½ months I didn't have any feelings for her. In fact, for tha whole plane ride I was thinking about Liz.

"What are you smiling about? I know you hear me Amir!"

"All that yelling isn't needed or called for."

"Well, you act like you couldn't hear me."

"Yeah Amir, she only asked you three times."

"My fault, my mind was elsewhere."

"I see."

"What was tha question?"

"Never mind."

"Mayla, she was spoiled coming up, wasn't she?"

"Silver spoon."

"I thought so."

"What's that supposed to mean?"

"When ever you can't get ya way or something doesn't go tha way you want it to you pout."

"I do not," she said poking her lips out.

"Case closed point proven. Ha! Ha! Ha!"

"I don't see nothing funny."

We all had suites next to one another and they were definitely first class. I had a message on tha phone, so I checked it.

"Hey Playboy, I knew you would be at this hotel hit me up on this number when you get in."

"Oh yeah, I'll have my sisters show tha girls around, so they won't be in our way."

"Now who's leaving you a message all tha way in Hawaii?"

"My people's Katul."

"Oh, so this was a front for a biz-ness trip? No wonder they love ya work it's coming all tha way from Hawaii."

"You trippin'!"

"I knew this was a biz-ness deal."

"This ain't no mafuckin biz-ness deal."

"Believe me if it was y'all would not be here."

"You smoove I'll give you that."

"Like I said you trippin' now let me hit my man up."


"UMM, UMM, YEAH RIGHT THERE! OOOOHH BABY YOU HITTIN' MY SPOT!"

"This how you like it?"

"YEEEES BABY YEEEEES! I'M CUMMING OOOOH BABY CUM WIT ME!!!"

"OH SHIT, OH SHIT I'M CUMMIN TOO!!!" Three seconds later our semen was one.

"I hope I don't get knocked up."

"This is tha first time we went raw you should be OK."

"I hope so."

"I told you to let me get a condom but no..."

"It was tha heat of tha moment."

"That and you was still horny from tha airplane."

"Yeah that too."

"Jazz you might need to get on tha pill."

"Why is that?" she asked wit a smile.

"Because that felt so good."

"It always does."

"Yeah but it really felt good hittin it raw."

"I must agree wit you on that."

"Wow."

"What?"

"You're actually agreeing wit me on something, that is definitely got to be a first."

"Boy shut up."

"Come on let's jump in tha shower."


"Tex can I ask you something?"

"You can ask me anything you want Mayla."

"A'ight, where is this going?"

Damn she caught me off guard wit that one my only response was, "Where is what going?"

"Us, me and you."

"I don't know what answer you lookin' for."

"For tha record, I'm only looking for tha truth Tex."

"Well in that case, Mayla I don't know where this is going."

"I know we said we would let it run its course and we have for tha last 10 ½ months."

"Mayla where are you going wit this?"

"I'm just gonna be honest and say it."

"Say what?"

"Tex I love you." I just stood there.

"Don't just stand there say something." I still didn't say shit, I just lifted her up and carried her to tha bed.

For tha next hour, I really put it on her wit out a condom.

We were just lying there when Mayla said, "So does this mean you feel tha same way?"

"Listen, Mayla I haven't lied to you before so I'm not going to start now. I don't know what I'm feeling but I do know I feel something for you."

He didn't have a chance to say tha actual words, but from that statement I knew what it was, so I straddled him and gave him tha ride of his life.

"Damn Stylz, you act like you had to prove something."

"Nah, I just wanna make sure I please you."

"Babe you always do."

I've been wit Stylz for 18 months and that was tha first time we had unprotected sex and Damn that Shit was tha bomb.

"We better get showered before ery body starts to get worried."

"They probably doing tha same thing we just did."

"Yeah you probably right."

Mayla, Roxy, and Jazz would find out over tha next few months that they were all pregnant. When tha plane landed back in Philly ery body was exhausted.

"Thank you Tex, I really enjoyed myself."

"I'm glad you did and so did I."

"I think we all did," Roxy said wit a big smile on her face.

"That was my first time going on a vacation and it definitely won't be my last, will it Fourty?"

"Nah, as long as you got money to travel."

"You ain't said nothing, I got my own money."

"I'm just playing wit you, no need to get hostile."

"Oh trust me, this is far from hostile." I didn't respond I just went to baggage claim.


"Damn Playboy, Jazz is real feisty."

"I don't pay her no mind."

"She really likes you."

"She told me she loves me."

"What did you say?"

"I kept it real, I told her I didn't know what I felt but I felt something."

"Ery body must have been on that lovey-dovey shit Mayla told me tha same thing."

"And?"

"My response was tha same as yours."

"Baby there goes tha luggage."

"Fuck, sittin' here running my mouth I missed tha damn luggage!"

"Don't worry, I got it for you!" Amir yelled from tha other side.

"Good lookin Baby Boy."

Once we were all done getting our luggage we made our way to tha parking garage.

"I'll get up wit y'all later."

"A'ight, I'll see y'all tomorrow I got to handle some biz-ness."

"Nigga you going to see Liz."

"Yup sure am."

We all went separate ways.

# CHAPTER 17

## Twist Flipped Out

"Listen, we don't want no problems you got that."

"I know y'all don't want no Mafuck'n problems!"

"Nah, Buck Fuck this Bitch Ass Nigga!"

"Nah, Nah, Nah, chill out Twist."

"You should listen to ya boy Little Nigga." Twist looked at me and I could tell he was heated.

"Yo like I said this shit ain't no good, hit me wit my money or it's about to be a serious problem."

"Swish how much weed my man get?"

"He got a pound."

"A'ight, give him tha weed and he'll give you ya bread back."

When he gave me tha bag I knew it wasn't tha same weed but I didn't say anything.

"You must think shit sweet, Nigga you ain't get that from us!" He reached for his waist line.

"Whoa, Whoa, hold up ain't no need for that, Swish give tha nigga his doe."

"Yo what tha Fucks up wit you Buck?"

"He ain't no fool and if you were smart you might thank him for just saving your sorry ass life!"

"Nigga fu..." Before Twist could finish I cut him off.

"There you go and please take ya biz-ness elsewhere from this point on."

"You don't have to worry about that." Once they were gone Twist flipped out.

"Buck what tha Fuck you let that nigga beat us for that change and weed."

"Man, this doe made you soft."

"Ain't nothing soft about me but my leathers I rock in tha winter."

"Well, you should've let me peel his potato."

"You can."

"How when you let him leave?"

"I got Lil Shep following them."

"Fuck that, we should've dead him and his boys right here on tha spot!"

"Nah, Twist we don't do it like that no more we move smart." I had to admit Buck was really thinking like a smart man.

"Buck I'm just not going to ever get use to people talking fly to us."

"It's hard for me too but we have to be smart. We'll see that nigga in a few hours trust me."

"I can't wait, Imma see how much he got to say then."


A few hours later, we were pulling up to this shabby red brick house.

"You sure he's there by his self?"

"Yeah, Lil Shep been sittin' on him all day since he left."

"I'll hit tha back you hit tha front."

"Same way we always do it." (BOOM! BOOM!)

"What tha Fuck?"

"Don't move you Bitch Ass Nigga!"

"You two will never get away wit this."

"That's tha same thing I was thinking earlier when you tried that

Bullshit."

"Yeah, and here we are in ya living room about to put an end to ya worthless life."

"How about I give back ya doe and we call it even?"

"Ha! Ha! Ha! I didn't know he was a comedian Buck."

At tha mention of Bucks name he looked like he saw a ghost. I had to look around to make sure nobody was behind me.

"Hold on, are you Fourty's nephew?"

"Does it matter Mafucka?"

"Yes."

"Nigga it didn't matter when you was poppin' fly earlier, so it damn sure don't matter now!"

"Let's do this Old Ass Nigga."

"Now what would Ms. Classy have to say about this?"

"What tha Fuck did you say Nigga?"

"Classy is ya mom, right?"

I put my .45 in his face and let him know if he even uttered her name again I will put his brains all over tha wall like a Picasso original.

"Shaheem I'm ya pop."

"Nigga my pop dead, he was killed before I was born."

"Ha! Ha! Ha! Is that what she told you?"

"I visit my pops grave every Father's Day, birthday, and when ever I need to talk or tell somebody my darkest secrets."

"That nigga ain't ya pop." I cocked tha trigger.

"Call ya mom and ask her."

I pulled out my phone and called but kept getting her voicemail.

"Damn!"

"Call Unc up."

"Oh yeah." After two rings he picked up.

"What tha deal wit you Nephew?"

"Unc I need to ask you something, but I need you to be totally honest wit me." I could tell it was something serious by tha tone in his voice.

"Talk to me Buck."

"Who is my dad and is he alive?"

"Where is this coming from?"

"This nigga saying, he my pops."

"What nigga?"

"What is your name Nigga?"

"Tell 'em it's Castro." Hearing his name brought rage in me like nothing else.

"Buck where you at?"

"Twist see what this address this."

"2402."

"2402 Cecil B Moore Avenue."

"Hold tight, I'm on my way and please keep him alive until I get there." I don't know what is going on, but I know my uncle is pissed.

Twenty minutes later, Fourty was coming through tha door followed by Tex, Stylz, and Amir.

"Well, Well, Well, if it isn't Castro."

"Nigga you should've stayed in hiding."

"You know he love other folks money."

"Yeah, never was tha type to get his own always waiting for tha next nigga."

"Can somebody fill me in?"

"Why don't you do tha honors Castro?"

"Like I told you I'm ya dad not that piece of shit you think is ya pop!"

"Mafucka don't you ever in ya filthy life disrespect Shaheem!"

(SMACK, SMACK, SMACK)

"Unc hold up."

"Mafucka do you know how much pain you caused my sista for years? Tha only person who could bring her back was Shaheem."

"Fuck Shaheem!" (SMACK)

"If he was alive he would kill you!"

"Mafucka who you think killed him?"

"Nigga you ain't built like that," Amir said walking up on Castro.

"Nigga I'm tha same nigga who sent ya Bitch Ass pop to tha bone yard wit two to tha back of tha head execution style." (POP! POP!)

Amir hit him in both knee caps.

"AAHHH SHIT!"

"Unc what tha Fuck is going on?"

"This nigga broke into ya mom and Shaheem's house, tied Shaheem up then raped ya mom."

"What?"

"Ya mom ended up pregnant, she didn't know who tha father." Tears wanted to come down my eyes, but I refuse to let them.

"That explains why sometimes I would catch her crying, but she would just say it was because she missed my dad."

"Shaheem told ya mom regardless what tha blood test showed he would love you unconditionally but unfortunately, he was killed before you were born."

"Yeah thanks to this Piece of Shit! I hope he sees you again!" (POP! POP! POP! POP! POP! POP! POP! POP! POP! POP! POP! POP! POP! POP! POP! POP!) "that's for my mom and my dad!" Buck emptied his whole clip in Castro's head almost disfiguring it from his body.

(CLICK, CLICK, CLICK)

"It's empty Buck." He snatched my gun. (BOOM! BOOM! BOOM!)

"Buck!" I yelled bringing him out of his daze.

When he turned around he had a long tear rolling down his eye.

"That bastard raped my mom."

"We been looking for Castro for tha past 15 years."

"Yeah, how did you find him?"

"He found me."

"How?" I explained what went down wit Castro.

"Damn Buck, I'm proud of you a year ago he would've been dead on tha spot."

"Money make you smart."

"Well, y'all got plenty of it now."

"Unc I wanna be tha one to tell my mom."

"You don't have to tell her anything."

"Nah, I think it'll make her feel a lot better."

As soon as I heard Tupac's "DEAR MAMA" I knew it was my mom.

"This her calling me now... Hello."

"Hey you called me?"

"Yes."

"I was under tha dryer and I didn't hear my phone."

"Mom I need to talk to you but not over tha phone."

"Wow, this must really be that important."

"It is."

"I'm on my way to tha house."

"I'll meet you there."

"Call tha cleanup crew Imma go wit Buck to tell Classy."

"You don't have to."

"I know I don't have to but I am."

"I'll call tha cleanup crew and get wit y'all later, I have to go see Liz."


When we pulled up to tha house this old lady was standing out front.

"Hello, can we help you?"

"Yeah, I'm looking for my granddaughter's house."

"What's her name?"

"Cindy."

"Oh Ms. Cindy lives next door."

"Thank you, Baby."

"No problem." Mom had Musiq Soulchild playing on tha stereo when I walked in.

"Hey."

"Hey Sis."

"This must really be serious if Fourty came wit you."

"You might want to turn tha radio off and sit down for this Sis."

"I really don't like tha sound of this, hold on let me get a glass of wine."

"I really don't like tha sound of this, hold on let me get a glass of wine."

"Yeah, I think you might need it." When she came back she had a glass and a whole bottle of wine.

"Mom I know what that Bastard did to you."

"Who, what Bastard?"

"Castro." All that could be heard was tha sound of breaking glass from her dropping tha wine glass she was sipping from.

"Fourty why did you tell him?"

"Mom he had no choice." She had a puzzled look on her face, so I explained tha story to her.

"So, you mean to tell me he tried to rob you?"

"Yup, but I had somebody follow him."

"Where did ya uncle come into play?"

"He said that he was my pop and if I didn't believe him call you. When you didn't answer I called Unc, who told me he would be right there. Him, Stylz, Tex, and Amir showed up. Mom I have never seen Unc so upset in my life."

"Classy that Mafucka told Amir he killed his dad too."

"No he didn't."

"Yes he did, he told Amir exactly how he was killed and unless you did it you wouldn't know."

"Oh My God."

"Mom Amir shot him in both his knees; he even had tha nerve to disrespect my dad."

"So Fourty did you?"

"No Mom I did, I emptied my whole clip plus three from Unc's gun in his head." Her mouth just hung open for a sec before she asked me if I was OK.

"Yeah I'm good."

"Are you sure?"

"Mom I'm straight."

"Damn you act like this isn't tha first time you killed somebody." Fourty looked at me and nodded.

"It's not that, I just don't feel anything because of what he did to you and I would do it again in a heartbeat. Mom nobody and I mean nobody will ever hurt you again and if they do they won't be around to talk about it! I love you Mom."

"I love you too Shaheem, but I would never want you to risk ya life for mines; a parent should never outlive their child."

"Excuse me I need to use tha bathroom."

"What am I going to do wit him?"

"Let him be tha man he's becoming and trust me he has come a long way."

"Alex what was my son doing in tha streets before he got involved in tha game?" I stood at tha top of tha stairs listening and waiting to hear about uncle's response.

"Classy he wasn't doing nothing teenage boys don't do."

"You would tell me, wouldn't you?"

"Ain't nothing to tell Sis."


"Unc you need a ride back, I gotta handle some biz-ness?"

"Yeah, let me get a ride."

"Mom did Sasha call you?"

"Yes she did."

"Well, I'll talk to you later on."

"OK you be careful out there."

"Always do plus Twist got my back."

"Tell him he need to stop by and visit his nana she's been worried about him."

"A'ight all make sure he goes by there to see her."

"You do that."


"Unc good lookin' in there."

"Come on Nephew you know I got ya back."

"I know how tight you and mom are, so I know you didn't want to lie to her."

"I didn't lie to her I just didn't tell her you probably got just as many bodies as a funeral home if not more."

"Ha! Ha! Ha! Damn Unc you giving me more credit than I deserve."

"Nah, you and Twist was racking them up. Y'all jumpin' in tha game is tha best thing that could happen to tha city. I had people callin' me and telling me to put a muzzle on you two niggaz."

"You never did."

"If I would have tried all that would have done was make y'all go even harder. Right or wrong?"

"Right."

"I know I am."

"Unc I need to re-up."

"A'ight, just give me a call when you ready."

"That's tha thing, I'm ready now."

"Well, we can handle it now if you want to."

"I just need to stop by one of my stash houses to grab tha money."


"Hey stranger."

"Hey Ma."

"I was starting to think you found a new toy to play wit."

"Toy? You're not a toy."

"You know how you have a toy then when you get a new one you stop playing wit tha old one."

"Liz you're far from my toy, I actually love you."

"Did I hear you correctly?"

"Yes you did."

"Repeat that again."

"I said I love you."

"Wow you got me blushing, I don't know what to say."

"There's nothing that needs to be said."

"Well, if I'm allowed to ask, when did this start?"

"About 3 months ago."

"And I'm just now hearing about it?"

"I needed to make sure I was actually feeling those feelings."

"What made you sure?"

"What's this 21 questions?"

"No, I'm sorry."

"You good, I'm just messing wit you."

"I knew for sure when I went away and couldn't stop thinkin' about you."

"Well, if you would've took me and not that other chick," Liz was smiling from ear to ear, "because I know," she said wit out me having to ask.

"You mad?"

"Not mad just jealous."

"That's what I love about you Liz you're always honest."

"Amir I'm 43-years-old I don't have time for games that was my younger days."

"Damn, you 43? I thought you was 28."

"You keep on making me blush."

"I'm dead serious, you don't look a day over 28; when you hit 60 you're gonna look 40 if not younger."

"Amir you're doing it again."

"That's all I know how to do is tell tha truth."

"I was talking about making me blush. Amir we always keep it 100 so I need to ask you a serious question."

I hope she's not going to ask me to just be wit her, I don't think I'm ready to completely commit to just one woman yet.

"Do you want to move in wit me? Hold on, before you answer that I'm not telling you that you still can't do you. Because I know when you're ready you will."

"I thought I was already living here."

"Not officially."

"You sure you want me here every night?"

"Positive."

"I got a much better idea."

"I'm listening."

"How about we find another house and we move in there."

"What am I going to do wit this? I just paid it off."

"Rent it out."

"That's not a bad idea."

"I have a lot of properties all over Philly, so we can start checking them out tomorrow."

"I'm off tomorrow anyway that works out great. If they're anything like this."

"Liz, this is probably tha worst one of my properties."

"Why didn't you show me anymore?"

"How could I when you were sold on this one?"

"Yeah, I guess you're right; I did instantly fall in love wit this one. Well, if you say this is tha worst I can't wait to see tha others. What time you coming back?"

"Who said I was leaving?"

"In that case, what do you want for dinner?"

"I was thinking we could go out to eat and then do a little dancing."

"Wow, you already got me no need to do all that."

"Liz, I've never been involved in a relationship, but I do know as long as you keep it romantic and exciting then it'll probably last for many years."

"To be only 22 you know a lot. Somebody been schooling you?"

"Nah, I just pay attention to my dad's parents, they been married for 52 years."

"Wow, that's true love."

"Tha funny thing is, they act like newlyweds."

"That probably so adorable."

"I wanna be like that one day."

"You can, you just have to find that one who makes ya heart skip a beat every time she enters tha room. Or when she leaves you can't wait for her to return."

"I feel like that now," I said looking her in her pretty gray eyes.

I could tell Amir was being sincere and it made me blush.

"I'll know when you're ready for that commitment and so will you."

"How?"

"Trust me, you will know."

# CHAPTER 18

## Pictures and Recordings but Still Nothing

"So, tell me you got something good for me Agent Sharp."

"I got these pictures and recording."

After tha Chief looked at them and listening to tha tapes he said, "These are useless."

"These guys have a direct link to Amir, Stylz, Tex, and Fourty so after we snatch them up, I know that one of I know that one of them if not all will be more than willing to talk."

"I didn't look at it like that."

"Chief you trust me, don't you?"

"Of course I do."

"I'm not doing all this work for nothing."

"I trust your judgment Agent Sharp so continue doing what you're doing."

"I will Chief."

"My superiors are pleased as well, this is tha closest we've ever come to getting an indictment on Amir and his crew."

"Don't worry Chief he won't get away this time."

"That's what I want to hear Agent Sharp, if you need anything else just ask."

"I could use a few mini cameras."

"How many?"

"At least 4."

"No problem."

"I'll call you in a few weeks."

"Ok be safe and watch your back."

After my meeting wit tha Chief I decide to go home for some must needed rest.

*"Oh Shit, I don't want to be seen leaving tha Federal building,"* she thought to herself.

"Buck is that Home Girl?"

"Who?"

"I don't know her name."

"Where she at?

"Right there."

"Nah, I don't know her."

"From a distance I thought it was tha chick that be wit ya uncle and them."

"Who Jazz?"

"Yeah that's her name."

"What would she be doing coming out of tha Federal building?"

"I don't know? Maybe she works there."

"Shit that was close, this is one time I don't mind somebody having tha same outfit as me. They don't know me anyway I could've told them anything. Let me get outta here before somebody else sees me."

"Listen you still owe me for tha last shipment you came up short on."

"I know, and I got it for you."

"Check this out, Sam if you keep doing it like this I'm never going to get my money."

"I hit you every time I re-up."

"Yeah but all I'm doing is fronting you work. So, if we gon' do it like that then I'll front you what ever you buy."

"A'ight, if that's how we gon' play it. I respect that Tex."

"You really don't have a choice."

"Well, let me get a whole bird."

"Damn you been using me to stack ya money."

"Yeah, I'm trying to get my weight up."

"Looks like you got it up Playboy."

"Not yet but I'm getting it there."

"Keep Fucking wit me and I'll have you sittin prettier than a drop top Maybach."

"Now that's what I'm talking about Baby Boy."

"Imma even lower tha price on tha one you're buying but tha numbers tha same on tha other one."

"That's good Shit."

"Sam, I like you that's why if you move this fast enough Imma turn it up a notch."

"Don't worry Tex Imma run through this like an NFL running back."

"Say no more, just hit me up when you ready. I got you."


"Hello."

"Hey Amir, are you busy?"

"Nah, not really."

"Do you want to catch a movie or something?" Even though I really didn't I said yeah anyway.

"A'ight, I'll pick you up in 30 minutes."

"Are you home?"

"Yes."

"Well, I'll pick you up then."

"No problem."

"Matter of fact, I gotta better idea."

"I'm listening."

"Tha boy Rafeeq outta Wilmington has this play called Why Men Do tha Things They Do."

"Oh yeah, I heard about it from my co-workers. They said it's real good."

"I know I've seen it once."

"Well it must be good for you want to see it again."

"It is, and it starts in a few hours so that should give you enough time to change."

"Don't you need tickets? They said it was all sold out."

"Paradise, I know a few people, not a lot but tha ones I do know matter."

"Excuse me, I forgot I'm dealing wit a boss."

"I'm not a boss."

"Well, what do you call ya self?"

"Amir."

"I guess, well I'll be ready by tha time you get here."

"Imma jump in this pond, get fresh then I'll be by to scoop you."

"A'ight, I would say call when you get close but I'm sure I'll hear you."

One hour later, I was pulling up to Paradise's house.

"MY CHICK BAD LOOKING LIKE A BAG OF MONEY, MY CHICK BAD LOOKING LIKE A BAG OF MONEY I GO AND GET IT THEN I LET HER COUNT IT FOR ME."

*"Wow, "* is what I thought when Paradise came walking out her house.

"Hello Handsome."

"Hello to you."

"I guess you got on tha same color as me."

"I can change, I had no idea you would be wearing a peach Roberto Cavalli Sundress wit matching sandals."

"So, you know your designers."

"Of course, my picture is probably next to fashion in Webster's."

"Boy you a mess."

"Oh yeah, thanks for tha compliment."

"What compliment?" She pointed to tha radio, all I could do was smile and push play.

"MY CHICK BAD LOOKING LIKE A BAG OF MONEY, MY CHICK BAD LOOKING LIKE A BAG OF MONEY I GO AND GET IT THEN I LET HER COUNT IT FOR ME."


When we pulled up to tha Queens in Wilmington it was packed.

"Damn, ery body wants to see this play."

"Yeah, they definitely came out."

"They will not be disappointed that's for sure."

"Well, I'm glad I didn't wear what I was gonna wear."

"Paradise you could've put on a sweat suit and still looked good."

"Yeah right."

- 137 -

I lucked up on a parking spot as somebody was pulling out.

"Look at you looking all sharp Mr. Ralph Lauren."

"Hey, I do my best."

I let Paradise walk in front of me, so I could see how she filled that dress out and boy did she fill it out.

"Amir are you going to look at my ass or walk wit me?"

"I can't help it Damn."

"Don't worry you'll have all night to look at it wit out tha dress on." I handed tha lady at tha door our tickets and we made our way to our seats.

"Amir."

"What up Rafeeq?"

"I can't call it."

"This must be your wife."

"Yeah Amir this is my wife Unika."

"Hello."

"Hey."

"This is my peoples Paradise."

I felt some type of way about Amir calling me his peoples, but I didn't let it show. I know I said I wouldn't let my feelings get involved but I was falling for him hard. I knew I had to reevaluate what ever this was I refuse to be hurt.

"Mayla you'll never believe this shit."

"What's up Roxy?"

"I'm pregnant."

"Bitch me too."

"Yeah right."

"Ten weeks."

"Shut up so am I"

"Hawaii," they both said in unison.

"Jazz called me this morning and said she's also ten weeks."

"Damn, I wonder if Paradise is knocked up too?"

"I hit her a little while ago, but she was in Wilmington wit Amir."

"Wilmington?"

"Yeah at some play."

"Why Men Do What They Do?"

"Is that by tha boy Rafeeq?"

"Yeah."

"It's Why Men Do tha Things They Do."

"I knew it was something like that."

"I told Tex I wanted to see that play."

"If it's anything like his books I know it's off tha chain."

"You know I just read his book Betrayal and Deceit."

"Giiiirl, Zoey's cousin Jibbs ain't Shit."

"I knew he was a snake when he was dealing wit Roscoe after she said Quez said they were shady and not do biz-ness wit them."

"Bitch I can go on and on about his books."

"He definitely can write, and he leaves you wondering for most of tha book."

"Bitch I still can't Fuckin believe we all pregnant."

"Who you telling; did you tell Tex yet?"

"No, I just found out yesterday."

"I told Stylz, he was happier than a punk in boys town."

"Bitch you stupid."

"He was, you know he don't got no kids."

"Neither does Tex, but we both said we didn't want any kids yet."

"So, what are you saying?"

"I'm thinking about not telling him and just getting an abortion."

"Mayla you can't just do that wit out telling him because his whole attitude might change."

"I don't want no kids."

"Well, you should have thought about that before having unprotected sex!"

"Bitch it was in tha heat of tha moment, she should know about that."

"Well, I still think you should give him tha option."

"I don't know."

"If he finds out you got an abortion wit out telling him your relationship will be over for sure."

Believe me Roxy I thought about all that but at tha end of tha day I have to do what's best for Mayla."

"You're right, just don't make a decision you might regret wit out really thinking it over."

"I will but in tha meantime don't tell Stylz."

"You think I tell Stylz everything?"

"Yes, I do think y'all tell each other everything."

"Well, you are dead wrong," I said lying.

"Yeah what ever, just keep ya mouth shut."

"What ever Bitch!"

"Roxy I'm dead serious."

"Mayla I got you."

"So, what do y'all want a boy or girl?"

"Well, I want a boy and Stylz wants a girl."

"Wow it's usually tha other way around."

"I know that's crazy, but at tha end of tha day I just want a healthy baby."

"I know that's right. So, when is tha wedding?"

"Wedding?"

"Yeah wedding, it is evident you two are Beyoncé and Jay-Z."

"Mayla what tha Hell are you talking about?"

"Bitch crazy in love."

"Oh Shit, Girl you crazy."

Roxy had her heart broken so much in tha past she deserves to be happy.

# CHAPTER 19

## Liz Admits She Loves Amir

"Liz you really like Amir."

"Like? Nah Sis, I love me some Amir."

"Does he know you feel this way?"

"Yes, and he feels tha same way."

"How long have tha two of you been messing around anyway?"

"Since he showed me my house."

"Now that was at least 18 months ago."

"That explains a few things."

"A few things like what?"

"Y'all living together and that tattoo you have across ya back."

"How do you know about my tattoo?"

"When you came by last week you bent over to pick up something and I saw it."

"Oh, that young boy put it on you."

"Yes he did and is still putting it on me."

"Damn Sis, I need to get me one of them young boys."

"Joanne I've never felt this way about another man like I do Amir."

"He's a lot mature than his age I know that."

"Age is nothing but a number."

"OOOOH I think I'll look good in this, don't you?"

"Yeah if you going to church."

"Liz not all of us has a body like yours."

"Joanne if you stop dressing like an old lady I'm sure you would have them beating ya door down."

"Old lady? Liz I am old."

"Please you only 45, that's hardly old."

Depends on who you ask."

"Let me help you out, come on."

"Where are we going?"

"To tha Gucci store."

"That's outta my price range."

"You need to treat ya self and stop being so cheap."

"I'm not being cheap."

"Yes you are, you can afford it."

"I don't need all that designer stuff to get a man."

"Joanne you need to do something maybe that's tha problem."

"What is tha problem?"

"You need some sex to loosen you up."

"I get that any time I want it."

"I'm not talkin' bout nothing wit batteries, I'm talkin' bout tha real deal."

"I like this dress," I said changing tha subject.

"Go try it on."

"It will fit it's my size."

"This is Gucci ya size may not fit."

"Which way is tha dressing room?"

"Over there, Imma pick you out a few more things to try on."

"A'ight."

"I should have been gave Joanne this makeover." When she came out wit that dress on I couldn't believe my eyes.

"Damn Sis, you got more ass than me."

"Liz, I have to admit I look Damn good in this dress."

"Yes you do, here go try this stuff on too."


A good two hours and about $6,000 later, my sister had a new wardrobe that consisted of Gucci, Prada, Chanel, Louis Vuitton, Liz Claiborne and Michael Kors. Then she spent another $4,800 on shoes.

"This should hold me down until next week."

"Hold on, is this tha same woman just 2 ½ hours ago said she doesn't need all that designer stuff to get a man?" was tha words I used, "you feel like a new woman in those clothes, don't you?"

"Yes I do, I think I might go have a few drinks tonight."

"Now that doesn't sound too bad I might just join you.

"Is Amir going to let you have a few drinks wit ya Sis?"

"Of course he will."

"You sure?"

"We don't have that type of relationship matter of fact, he'll probably ask if he can come wit us."

"Yeah, I doubt that."

"Watch." I called Amir's phone and put it on speaker, after four rings answered.

"Hey Ma"

"Hey Baby."

Everything a'ight?"

"Yeah, I was just calling to let you know ya plate will be in tha microwave when you get in."

"You gonna be sleep."

"No, I'm going to tha bar wit Joanne to have a few drinks."

"Your sister Joanne?"

"Yup."

"Wow, this is a first."

"I know right."

"Is it just tha two of y'all?"

"Yes why?"

"Ask Ms. Joanne would she mind if I tag along."

I looked at Joanne's wit a look that said I told you.

"No, I don't mind Amir."

"You got me on speaker?"

"Yeah because she said you wouldn't let me go and I told her you would want to go wit us."

"Oh, so you know me?"

"After 18 months, I would say I think I do."

"What time y'all leaving?"

"About 8 o'clock."

"I have a better idea."

"I'm listening."

"There's a party my people Rafeeq is throwing at tha Chase Center in Wilmington tonight."

"Tha one who's play we went to?"

"That's tha one."

"I'm game."

"Make sure you're ready no later than 9 o'clock."

"I'll be ready at tha house."

"Me too."

"Well, Joanne needs to make sure she's ready by 9 o'clock."

"I'll be ready, you just make sure you're on time."

"Baby I'll meet you at tha house."

"Amir don't be long, maybe we can get it in before we get dressed."

"Liz, they say great minds think alike."


"You two are something else."

"That's my baby, I love him so much Sis."

"That would definitely explain tha glow you've had for tha past year."

"Joanne, I know he's a lot younger than me, but you would never know it by tha way he carries himself."

"I like him, he's always very respectable when he comes in tha store."

"I don't think Amir has a disrespectful bone in his body. Sis he has one amazing body."

"I'm sure he does."

"Before I got wit him I was lucky to just have one orgasm; now I'm so accustomed to having multiple orgasms and I get mad if I only get two."

"Liz you are crazy."

"Joanne I'm not lying, that young boy puts it down in tha bedroom."

"Damn, you got tha whole package."

"Yes I do, and I am loving it too."

"UNH, UNH, UNH, must be nice."

"Yes it is, you just don't know."

"I think I might need to invest in one of those myself."

"Invest in what?"

"A young boy."

"Tha right one will bring your youth back for sure."

"Well, we better be going if we plan to be ready by 9 o'clock."

"I'll be ready."

"Well, you know I'm slow."

"Come cause I would hate for you to miss out on tha chance to meet ya self a young boy."


After droppin' Joanne off I headed to tha house to get dressed.

"Amir are you home?"

"Yeah Babe I'm upstairs about jump in tha shower."

"Oooh No you're not."

"Why not?"

"Because you about to dig my back out."

"I thought you changed ya mind as long as you was taking."

"I had to help Joanne get a new wardrobe."

"You did what?"

"I had to help her step her dress game up."

"Wow, I know that cost her some paper."

"Almost $11,000."

"Daaaamn!"

"You know how I do it."

"She went for that?"

"Baby once she tried on that first Gucci dress it was a wrap."

"I really can't imagine Ms. Joanne in Gucci."

"She doesn't want you to call her Miss anymore."

"Let me found find out Stella gettin' her groove back."

"I been had my groove back, matter fact, I never lost my groove."

"I'm not talkin' about you I was talking about Ms. Joanne."

"Didn't I tell you not to call her Ms. anymore?"

"I'm used to calling her that."

"Enough of tha chit chat, come give Mommy some," I said slippin' outta my Chanel dress." As soon as he dropped his boxes I instantly got wet.


45 minutes later, we were in tha shower washing one another up.

"That ought to hold me down til later."

Once we were dressed we made our way to Joanne's. (BEEP-BEEP) Amir hit tha horn twice.

"Oh Shit!"

"What?"

"Is that Ms. Joanne?"

"Ha! Ha! Ha! Boy you crazy, I didn't know what you were talkin' bout."

"She looks like a totally different person."

"Gucci will do that to a person."


"Hey Amir."

"Hello Ms. Joanne."

"Liz, I thought I told you to tell him to drop tha Ms."

"She did but it's a habit."

"Well, that's one habit you're gonna have to break starting tonight. I can't have you calling me Ms., especially when I'm trying to catch me a young boy."

"Awe shit, what has Liz been telling you?"

"Nothing."

"You answered that too fast, so I know she said something."

"I did, I told her that you were really mature and make me happy."

"Now you got me blushing."

"Just telling tha truth."

"Liz you know you my Baby."

"Ditto."

"Listen to you two, if I didn't know any better I'd think y'all were in love." We both looked at each other then smiled.

"Did I miss something?"

"No," we both said at tha same time.

"By tha way, Joanne you look nice."

"Thank you, Amir, you look pretty good ya self."

"Not to sound conceited but I know."

"For tha record, that does sound very conceited."


We arrived at tha Chase Center sent in Wilmington at 10 o'clock, it was packed.

"Damn that's a long line."

I pulled up in V.I.P. to let tha Valet park my Maybach. It's just so happens that Rafeeq was standing at tha door.

"Amir what up Baby Boy?"

"I can't call it."

"Damn you got two bad honey's wit you tonight."

"Nah, this my girl and her sister." That made me feel good to hear Amir call me his girl.

"Liz, Joanne this is my peoples Rafeeq."

"Hello Ladies."

"As-Salamu Alalkum."

"Walaikum Salam," I saw tha way Liz looked at me, so I said, "I read my share of books on Islam."

"Hum-Du-Lilahi."

"Let me get three V.I.P. tickets," Amir said pulling out his money."

"Come on now you disrespecting me, put ya money away."

"Alex let me get three V.I.P. bands."

"Here you go Amir."

"Thanks Rafeeq."

"You do tha same when I come to Philly."

"I'll see you later I gotta make a run."

"A'ight."

"For tha record, Joanne if I wasn't married I'd be on you." All I could do was smile.


"Come on let's take a few pictures first." We took enough for all of us to have our own.

"SEE HER IN THA CLUB SEE HER DO HER THING YOU MIGHT WANNA RAP, BUT SHE'LL MAKE YOU SING."

"Heeeey this my jam right here," Liz said as she started dancing.

"This song is old as Shit."

"So what, it's still my song."

"Excuse me would you like to dance?"

"I'm good wit him."

"I was talking to her," he said pointing at Joanne.

"Sure, why not." They hit tha floor and it was on.

"Look at ya sister she can dance."

"Runs in tha blood."

"Hmm I bet it does."

"Stop playin' you know I'm tha Shit on tha dance floor."

I couldn't front Liz was tha Shit on tha floor. She could actually keep up wit me and not too many women could. When they played that old juvy "BACK DAT ASS UP" Liz did just that. Before long, my Shit was rock hard.

"I need to sit down."

"You might want to wait til tha elevator goes down." She learned back to hide my hardness.

"OOOOH Damn, you know I don't got no panties on."

"Just like you know my Shit is rock hard so why would you back up on it like that?" She just gave me a devilish grin that said I want some.

"Are you thinking what I'm thinking?"

"Depends on what you thinking."

"Us, car."

"I was thinking that, but I was thinking bathroom."

"Come on."

"Where are y'all two sneaking off to?"

"He's walking me to tha bathroom."

"I know y'all not about to get it in in tha bathroom?"

"No."

"Yes y'all are."

"No we not."

"UNH, UNH, UNH, trifling."

"Stop hating."

"I'm not."

"We'll be back." I would never hate on my sister, but I was a little jealous.

"Hey Ma, can I buy you a drink?"

"Sure, why not."

"Let me guess, Long Island Ice Tea."

"Nah, try Cîroc wit a splash of cranberry."

"My bag, most females like that Long Island."

"I'm not Most females."

"I see."

"I never caught ya name."

"I never threw it."

"Damn Ma you don't stop. Well I'm Tyree."

"I'm Joanne."

"You could've fooled me, I just knew you were gonna say your name was Heaven, Angel, or Lovely." I had to smile at his attempt to run game.

"You're not from here, are you?"

"No, I'm not."

"I know because I've never seen you before tonight. If you don't mind me asking where are you from?"

"West Philly."

"Damn, this how they breeding 'em in West Philly?"

"I guess so."


"I see somebody has met a friend."

"Fix ya self."

"I thought I did."

"Hello I'm Liz."

"Hello I'm Tyree."

"He's a little cutie pie."

"Y'all have to be sisters."

"Why do we have to be sisters?"

"Y'all look-alike."

"Yeah that's my sister."

"Let me introduce you to my boy."

"Nah that's a'ight I have a man."

"What kind of man would let you come out by ya self?" his friend said walking up on me.

"He wouldn't," Amir said grabbing my waist. I could tell Tyree's friend didn't like it but hey to bad.

"My fault Playa."

"I don't blame you, if she wasn't my girl I'd be on her too."


"Tyree let's take a couple pictures."

"A'ight, Joanne would you like to take a few pictures?" I was about to say no but Liz gave me that look that said go ahead.

"Sure, why not."

"Ty you bucked up wit Shorty."

"Who you telling." I ended up taking three pictures wit Tyree and he let me have two of them.

"Maybe when I come visit I'll see them on ya mantelpiece."

"You real confident."

"I gotta be."

"You probably got all types of girls."

"Nah, I just got two friends, nothing serious." I definitely had to respect his honesty, so he got points for that.

"Joanne how about we exchange numbers, so I can let you do you, I don't want to cramp ya style."

"A'ight." After we exchanged numbers, he went his way and I went mines.

"Damn you ran tha young boy off."

"Nah, we exchanged numbers."

"You better had got his number."

"Where is Amir?"

"Over there talkin' to Rafeeq."

"I think that was so cute when he said he wouldn't let his girl come out by herself."

"I know right."

"Liz, he loves you I can see it in his eyes. Has he completely cut all tha other broads off?"

"No."

"Why not?"

"We have an understanding."

"Fuck an understanding."

"We established this from tha door."

"Yeah, that was before feelings got involved Liz."

"He's getting tired."

"How do you know that?"

"Because he's coming home damn near every night now to where before it would be one or two nights a week."

"If it works for you that's all that matters."

"Joanne, I'm 43-years-old so I have patience."

"Believe you me if I didn't think he would be wit just me I probably would have been stepped off."

"AS LONG AS YOU LOVE ME WE CAN BE STARVING, WE CAN BE HOMELESS, WE CAN BE BROKE AS YOU LOVE ME I'LL BE YA PLATINUM, I'LL BE YA SILVER, I'LL BE YA GOLD, JUST AS LONG AS YOU LOVE ME."

I felt someone grab me from behind, so I was instantly turned around only to be face-to-face wit Amir.

"What's wrong Liz?"

"Nothing."

"Something is wrong, I can see it on ya face."

"I just realized tonight how much I love you that's all."

"Why tonight?"

"You never called me your girl and you did twice tonight. I was beginning to think that I was over my head."

"Liz, you know you my number one."

"Now you making me blush."

"Liz, I love you. You do know that, right?"

"Yes I do." I said wit tha biggest smile my face could form.

Liz had no idea, but I was seriously thinking about settling down wit just her.


After dropping Joanne off we went straight home to finish where we left off at in tha bathroom. By tha time we were done tha sun was coming up.

"I'm turning my phone off I need some sleep and don't want to be disturbed."

"That sounds good but Imma jump in tha pond first."

"Me too." We ended up going another round in tha shower.

"Amir, I don't know what you've done to me, but you got a bitch strung out on you."

"Liz all I've done is keep it real wit you."

"Yes, you have and that's what really makes you so damn lovable."

"I like what we have."

"It's a'ight," I said being sarcastic.

"What you mean a'ight?"

"Just like I said Boy a'ight." I didn't respond after that I just let it go.

"Cat got ya tongue now?"

"Everything doesn't call for a response."

"Ha! Ha! Ha! Amir you funny. I'm going to bed will you be joining me?"

"Of course I will."

"It was one Hell of a night last night."

"What did you do?"

"Me and Sash went to tha movies and stayed at tha Embassy."

"Wow, you was feeling frisky last night I see."

"I need my own spot."

"Well, get one then."

"Man, you know mom don't wanna nigga to leave tha nest."

"Then I suggest you get a spot on tha low."

"I was thinkin' about that."

"Stop thinkin' and just do it."

"Imma tell Sash to look into it."

"One of my peeps got a few spots they trying to rent out."

"Nah, Imma just holla at Amir."

"Oh yeah, he does have all that property."

"And I could probably get for tha low."

"Low? Shit I think I need to get at Amir."

"Now you wanna get a spot."

"Nigga you know my moms been bugging about me living wit her."

"Why?"

"She said, since I want to be grown I need my own."

"Man, you lucky, I'll be happy if my mom lets me move out before I'm 30."

"Ha! Ha! Ha! Buck you stupid as Hell."

"Twist you know how my mom is."

"Anyway, did you holla at Fourty?"

"Yeah early this morning everything is a go."

"That's what's up."

"I was thinking about messing wit a little dope."

"Hell No!"

"Why not?"

"For one, we don't need tha money, for two that Shit gets you hotter than a summer day in Arizona."

"Nigga tha profit is serious."

"Hell Nah and that's all it is."

"A'ight if you say so."

"Twist I'm dead ass serious."

"A'ight I here you."

"You make sure you hear me, we don't need no heat on us we doing just fine."

"Ain't nothing wrong wit gettin' a little more money."

"Nigga we don't need it we ain't hurting."

"Yeah you right."

"Twist I must say you calmed down a whole lot since we started really gettin paper."

"Beef and money don't mix like milk and ketchup."

"Nigga you stupid as shit."

"EVERY TIME I SEE YA FACE IT MAKES ME WANNA SING, AND EVERY TIME I HEAR YA VOICE IT MAKES ME GO CRAZY."

"Hold up Twist."

"What up Sash?"

"Hey Baby, Keysha just asked if we wanted to go out to dinner and a movie wit her and Twist."

"I'm wit Twist now he ain't say nothing about it."

"She was about to call him."

As if on cue Twist phone started ringing. I could tell she must of been askin' him because he looked over at me. I just shrug my shoulders."

"Buck, Buck."

"Yo."

"Did you hear what I ask you?"

"No I didn't."

"I said do you want to go or not?"

"Sash I don't care it's up to you."

"Well, I'll call now and let her know we'll go."

"A'ight just hit me back wit tha time."

"What are you doing and why you rushing me off tha phone?"

"Now you trippin' cause ain't nobody rushing you off tha phone."

"Just making sure Big Head."

"Well you would know wouldn't you."

"Boy pleeeeeease, don't flatter ya self Mr. Inchworm."

"Ha! Ha! Ha! Anyway, I'll hit you back a little bit."

"Yeah you do that."


"They just do things wit out asking if we busy or not."

"Sash ask me if I wanted to go."

"I don't feel like doing no dinner or movie."

"Why, you got something else set up?"

"Nah, I just ain't for it tonight."

"Well, why didn't you tell Keysha that?"

"Because all she gonna say is we never do anything."

"You need to take pointers from Buck."

"What so bad about that? Nigga I don't need to take no mafuckin' pointers from you."

"So much hostility in your voice."

"Just because you be on that lovey dovey bullshit don't mean I have to be."

"Twist I don't be on that I just take her out once a week to keep her quiet."

"Damn I didn't look at it like that."

"Trust me, you do that she'll be happier than a faggot at a gay convention."

"Ha! Ha! Ha! Nigga you stupid as Hell."

"Ha! Ha! Ha!"

"Let me hit her back and tell her it's a go."

"See you can learn a thing or two from me tha same way I listened to my uncle when he was schooling me to tha game. Always know how and what to do to keep ya woman happy."

"I feel you. What's playing at tha movies anyway?"

"I wanna see that flick Premium Rush."

"Is that wit that dude on that bike trying to deliver a package or something?"

"Yeah that's it, tha previews looked a'ight."

"Ain't nothing else worth seeing."

# CHAPTER 20

## Amir and Allisa

"Listen up Mafucka you had two weeks to come up wit my money!"

"I-I-I-I kknow T-T-T-Tex but I-I-I-I don't h-h-have it y-y-yet."

"Well this isn't ya lucky day then."

"C-C-Come on M-M-Man all I n-n-need is another d-day or t-t-two."

"P-P-Please Nigga if you ain't got it now I know you ain't gonna have it in a day or two."

"I-I-I-I will I-I-I-I promise."

"You know what, Imma give you a week to get my paper."

"T-T-Thank you T-T-Tex."

"If you try to run I'll find you."

"I-I-I-I ain't r-r-running n-n-nowhere."

"Let him go Stylz." As soon as Tex let him go he headed straight for tha door.

"Tex you know he really did get robbed?"

"I know, I just want to see if he's gonna come up wit $50,000."

"He might skip town."

"That Nigga ain't going nowhere trust me."

"What if he comes up wit that money?"

"I'll hit him off."

"He's not comin' up wit that change."

"Probably not but he's gonna come to tha table wit something."

"Word on tha street Jasper and Kane are tha ones who did it."

"I know, I'm already on top of it."

"I know they knew that Sap had ya work."

"That was tha way I thought too, then I came to tha conclusion that they were just tired of living. If all goes according to plan, we'll have them by tomorrow night."

"Awe Shit."

"What?"

"You got that look on ya face."

"What look is that Stylz?"

"Death!"

"You're right on point wit that assumption."

"I been around you long enough to know."

"Ha! Ha! Ha!"

"So, you gonna put me down?"

"Of course, I thought you never ask."

After Tex schooled me I had to admit it was a brilliant plan as long as they went for it.

"Stylz them niggaz to greedy not to go for it. Throw a bone and a dog will fetch it every time."

"I think they gonna try it tonight."

"Well, I ain't got shit to do I'll be waiting on them."

"Well, I'm wit you on this one, Amir and Fourty said they want in on it too."

"We'll call them up and tell them to meet us there in an hour."

"Chief, I'm closing in on their whole team."

"All of them?"

"Yes."

"Agent Sharp you really are about to do what no one else has ever been able to do."

"I know, I know," I said wit a big Kool-Aid smile.

"This is going to earn you a nice promotion."

"Chief."

"Yes Agent Sharp."

"Never mind."

"What's on your mind Agent Sharp?"

I really wanted to tell Chief what was on my mind but all I could say was I didn't think I could do it.

"But you are and that's what matters." Tha truth was, I was really no closer than I was 18 months ago.

"Agent Sharp if you need anything don't hesitate to ask."

"Alright Chief."

"I'll let tha big wigs know how things are going in tha case."

"You do that." I slowly walked out of tha Chief's office.


"Hello Paradise."

"Hey Manny."

"You still not trying to give a brother no play?"

"I told you I don't date co-workers."

"What if I quit, would you date me then?"

"Boy you know damn well you ain't quitting this job."

"For a chance to date you it's possible."

"It sounds good."

"So, is that a yes?"

"Manny, we don't have nothing in common it wouldn't last."

"We won't know unless we give it a try."

"I'll take a rain check."

"You must have a man in ya life."

"Why can't I just not want to date you?"

"Come on Paradise, you know I'm a catch."

"For somebody else maybe."

"What's his name?"

"Who?"

"Tha Nigga you in love wit."

"Manny if you put as much effort in ya work as you do in pursuing me you'd be on top of ya game."

"Paradise you should know as well as anybody I'm good at my job."

"That's what ya mouth says."

"Not my mouth my actions."

"Well, I got work to do so I'll talk to you later."

"You just make sure you hurry up and rap that case up."

"What case?"

"That big lawsuit you been working on," he said winking.

"I will because tha payoff will be seven figures."


"Well, Well, Well, if isn't 'I wouldn't have took ya number if I wasn't going to call' hello Allisa."

"Amir you so full of shit! You could've called me."

"I didn't have ya number and my brother wouldn't give it to me."

"I'm sorry, I been so busy."

"Yeah, I'm sure you have been."

"Real talk, I got a lot going on."

"Well then I guess you still don't have time for me?" Seeing her standing there in that dress looking fat as ever gave me and instant erection.

"Allisa I'll be honest, I'm not looking for no girl."

"That's good cause I'm not looking for a man either, just as a friend wit benefits."

"What kind of benefits?"

"Both," she said looking at my pockets and penis."

"That works for me."

"Let's go then."

"Excuse me?"

"I said lets go unless you busy."

"Nah not at all."


25 minutes later we pulled up to tha Embassy.

"You sure you want to do this?"

"Amir, I know you not getting cold feet?"

"Nah."

"Well come on so I can throw this come back on you."

"Come back?"

"Yup, because you'll be back."

"Ha! Ha! Ha! Cocky and confident, I like that."

"Aren't you?"

"I let my work speak for itself."

"You just hurry up and get tha room, so we can handle our biz-ness."

As soon as we got to tha room Allisa jumped in tha shower. When she finished she quickly let me know that she didn't just have sex, but she wanted to make sure she wasn't sweaty since it was humid outside. I respected that because anybody else wouldn't have done that. When she let tha towel drop from her body I was in awe. Her clothes did her body no justice at all. Her Shit was flawless, and her Ass even looked bigger.

"Are you going to take your clothes off or do I need to help you?"

"Imma big boy I think I can handle it." As soon as I slid my boxers off Allisa's mouth dropped.

"Damn you hung like a horse."

"You can handle it."

Yup, sure can," she said wit confidence.

She took tha head a rubbed it on her clit to get her even more moist than she already was.


"OOOOOH YEEEEEE!," she yelled as she slid half of it inside her.

"I can handle it from here," I told her as I took control.

"AAAAAH SHIT!"

"You A'ight?"

"I will be as soon as I get adjusted," she said wit a big smile.

15 minutes later, she was well adjusted and doing her thing like a champ. I couldn't front, her Shit was definitely on point. I decided enough was enough and started putting it down something serious.

"YEEEEEES DAAADDY YEEEEEES!"

Tha more she tried to take control tha more I put it on her. I could tell she wasn't use to not being in control.

"OOOOOH SHIT! What are you trying to do to me?

"This is what you wanted ain't it?"

"YEES UMM OOOH SHIT! I'M COMING! OH MY GOD!" Once at her but I study to hit her spot.

"SHIT YEEES RIGHT THERE AMIR RIGHT THERE! OOOH I'M COMING AGAIN!"

Damn, Amir was definitely handling biz-ness, I'm lucky to nut once let alone four OOOH five times. By tha time he was done I had a total of 8 orgasms.

"I hope I didn't disappoint you."

"Boy you know damn well you did ya thing."

"I'm not gon lie, so did you and tha Shit is banging."

"Well thank you, it's not often you'll find a guy who will admit that call it a Macho thing. I have no problem giving props where props are due. And you definitely get my props."

"I haven't had anything that good since my old moms, so I probably will be coming back like you said."

"Ha! Ha! Ha!"

"What's so funny?"

"I know I'll definitely be back myself." I went to hit her wit some paper and she frowned.

"It's a stack that's not enough?"

"That's plenty, if I was going to take it."

"Huh?"

"Amir tha way you just put it down how can I take ya money?"

"I don't know if I should be honored or feel disrespected."

"Be honored, I've never had 9 orgasms before, Shit I barely get one let alone 9."

"I know you not done yet?"

"Shit I was hoping you wasn't, I thought you might have gave me ya all."

"Allisa that was only a warm up."

"That's what I'm talkin' about, let me jump in tha shower and I'm ready."

Allisa was very clean. When she jumped in tha shower I put tha money in her purse anyway. Just when I was thinking about settling down wit Liz. I kind of wish I would've been called her.

*Damn I can't believe he put it down like that. Not only is he hung but he knows how to use it. Most guys that are hung don't know what to do wit it and tha ones that do are inch worms. Let me get out, so I can get some more of that Shit he got in there. I had to laugh to myself because I knew this wouldn't end well at all.*

"Damn I thought you drowned in there."

"Nah, I just gotta make sure my Shit was right."

"Allisa how old are you?"

"Little too late for that question don't you think?"

"I know you older than 18."

"I'm 23."

"You older than Shaft?"

"Yup, by two years."

"He just acts like tha big brother."

"Yeah cause I just knew he was older."

"Well I'm ready, I came to get my back dug out not talk about my brother."

"I'm waiting on you."

"Say no more," she said getting on top of me backwards."

One hour later, we both lay there panting like two wild animals. Allisa saw me look at my watch.

"Don't let me hold you up."

"I was just checking to see if I had enough time to catch a nap."

"Not to brag but I've been known to put 'em to sleep afterwards."

"Ha! Ha! Ha! Is that right?"

"Absolutely."

"Do you need me to take you back?"

"Oh, you one of those Fuck 'em then send 'em on their way?"

"Come on, you might have other things to do besides stay here wit me."

"If I did you wouldn't have to say nothing I would've told you."

"My fault."

"And for tha record, I'm not a whore, smut, trick, or prostitute."

"Damn, where that come from?"

"No, I'm just saying I see you after God knows how long talk a little Shit then we end up here."

"Trust me, I know you're not none of those."

"What's that 'pose to mean?"

"Tex had put me down tha first time and let me know that I had to put work in to get in ya panties."

"That's why you didn't call?"

"Truth be told, nah I'm a busy man."

"Well, I guess I should feel honored to have your time right now."

"I would not go that far."

"Well, if you don't mind Imma get some sleep wit you."

"I've also been known to have that effect."

"Boy pleeeease."

"I've also been known to have 'em begging for more."

"Ha! Ha! Ha! You just don't stop."

"I'll deal wit you after I rest up."

"Let me find out you need rest."

"Pleeeease, like Foxy said my sex drive all night like a trucker."

"Well lets go then." I had to make a mental check list."

"Nice size tool-check, good sex-check, make me have multiple orgasms-check, knows how to work his tool-check, has stamina-check."

"Damn Amir is too good to be true too bad he's not looking for a girl." After tha first 9 I didn't think I had anymore left boy was I wrong."

"No wonder they go crazy for you."

"Believe it or not half of them have never had tha pleasure to be wit me."

"Stop lying."

"Real talk."

"Then why they act like that?"

"That's solely off tha conversation."

"Oh, so you mind Fuck 'em."

"If that's what you wanna call it keepin' it real wit 'em."

"Well, I know you have a girl, so I won't blow ya spot up."

"For tha record, I don't have a girl but..." I knew there was a but in there somewhere.

"I do have two friends."

"Let me guess, one is tha old moms you was talking about?"

"Yeah."

"What about tha other?"

"Keeping it real, she cool but I'm not really feeling her like that."

"So she's replaceable?"

"Tha way you just put it down Hell yeah."

"Good," she said laying on her tummy sticking her Ass in tha air."

"Well, what are you waiting for jump in." When I did she slowed her Ass literally.

"So, you was holding back on a brother?"

"Can't give you everything at one time you might not wanna come back if I do."

"Unlikely but I feel you though."

Damn Allisa was throwing that thing on me something serious. She definitely took Paradise spot or at least bumped her to tha third spot on tha roster. Hell, Liz better step her game up too. Nah, she can't take my baby's spot.

# CHAPTER 21

## Paradise Coming Out of tha Feds Building

"Aye Fourty isn't that Paradise coming out of tha Fed building?"

"Yeah that's her."

"Hey Paradise." I looked around to see who was calling me.

"Hey Fourty, Tex."

"What you doing?"

"I have a case against tha Feds and I'm trying to get them to settle out of court to avoid a long drawn out case."

"That's right take they money."

"Yeah Fuck tha Feds!"

"Who you telling I hate going in there dealing wit them Pigs."

"Is ya case beatable?"

"I got them by tha balls they just won't agree to tha 3.5 million we asking for."

"Damn that's a lot of money."

"Not really, if they take it to trial they will have to pay at least 8 or 9 million."

"So why won't they settle then?"

"They think we'll come down on our number."

"Fuck 'em P if they don't want to settle take all of their money."

"That's tha plan."

"So where y'all headed?"

"To lunch you wanna join us?"

"Sure, why not I was on my way to Ms. Tootsie's anyway."

"That's where we headed."

"I'll follow y'all then."

"Jazz and Mayla is suppose to meet us there too."

It was a little crowded when we arrived at Ms. Tootsie's. I spotted Jazz and Mayla as soon as I walked in.

"Paradise is over here," Mayla said wit her hand in tha air.

"Are you eating here or picking ya order up?"

"She's eating wit us," Fourty said before I could respond.

Before Mayla could ask I said, "I ran into them coming out tha Federal building."

"You still working on that same case?"

"Yes."

"Damn it's been a year."

"Longer than that."

"I know you ready for them to just settle, so you can get ya money."

"You damn right I'll be a Rich Bitch after that."

"So what's tha deal wit you and Amir?"

"I don't know he must got a New Bitch cause he been on some other Shit tha past few weeks."

"Bitch let me find out you done fell in love wit Amir."

I couldn't deny that I did fall in love wit him, but I wouldn't tell them that not in front of Fourty and Tex anyway.

"I don't know about love, but I do have feelings for him."

"You don't have to say that just because we here."

"Trust me I'm not," I said lying.

"You know I don't believe right."

- 173 -

"What ever Tex."

"Mayla she loves him."

"Tex if she said she don't than she don't end of story."

"Hold up, who you talkin to?"

"Didn't I say ya name?"

"You might wanna check tha attitude."

"I ain't gotta check Shit!"

"You know what you right."

"Fourty you can stay if you want but I'm out." He looked at Jazz who gave him tha nod of approval.

"Don't call me later either!" Mayla yelled.

"You'll call me before I call you!"

"I'm glad you think so."


"What was that about?"

"Man, she been on some bullshit lately."

"Maybe just maybe she wants a commitment that you're not willing to give her."

"On some real, she's too busy."

"Nigga you just ain't ready for a relationship."

"Truthfully, I am I need to settle down wit one woman."

"It's not easy, trust me."

"What made you do it?"

"I was tired of whoring and Jazz is pregnant."

"Say word."

"Word up."

"Why you just now telling me?"

"Nigga I just found out last night."

"She keeping it?"

"Of course she is."

"Congrats."

"I can't believe it, I'm going to be a father."

"Well believe it cause you are."


"Mayla you still haven't told Tex yet?"

"No."

"What are you waiting for?"

"Same thing you waiting on."

"I told Fourty last night."

"Was he happy?"

"Happy isn't tha word."

"Jazz I still haven't decided whether Imma keep it or not."

"Girl you 12 weeks, you better make up ya mind soon."

"I know, I know, I just don't think Tex wants or is ready for kids yet."

"It's about what you want. And tha question is, do you want a baby?" I had to take a minute to think about that question.

"Jazz I just made up my mind I'm keeping my baby."

"What about Tex?"

"What about him?"

"When you going to tell him?" I pulled out my phone and called him.


"Look at this shit, Fourty she is crazy."

"Hey Man."

"Hello Tex, we need to talk."

"I'm listening."

"Not over tha phone."

"Well, when then?"

"I'll call you when I'm on my way home."

"A'ight, can you order me a chicken and shrimp dinner?"

"Boy you got some nerve."

"Never mind, just hit me when you on ya way home."

"Mac and greens for tha sides, right?"

"Yes please, extra mac and shrimp."

"If I didn't love you."

"Well, I'm thankful you do and you're right we do need to talk, so I'll just meet you at ya house."

"Ok no problem."


*"This should be an interesting talk. Imma just let her know what needs and is going to happen. If she wants to be in a committed relationship wit me point blank. I can't wait to hear how this plays out. Either she gonna roll wit tha punches or Imma fall back from her."*

"Nigga you don't mean that."

"Yes I do, Mayla my baby but I don't have tha time or energy to keep doing this song and dance."

"So, if she agrees wit ya terms."

"Then she'll be wifey. Drop me off to my car and I'll hit you later and let you know what tha deal is."

After Fourty dropped me off I headed straight for Mayla's. We were both pulling up at tha same time.

"Damn, you came straight here?"

"You said we need to talk, and I have something to say as well."

"You might wanna eat while ya food is still hot."

"Is ya microwave not working?"

"My microwave works just fine."

"Well I'll just heat it up if it's cold. Do you wanna go first or should I?"

"You can go."

"A'ight, Mayla I don't know what tha deal is wit you lately wit all this bickering and fussing you been doing."

"But you're starting to push me away."

"I..."

"Hold up let me finish. I know that you want a commitment and that's probably part of tha reason you been so pissed at me. I do love you but if you continue to act tha way you're acting Imma be in tha wind like a kite."

"Are you finished?"

"Yes I am."

"Hold on let me use tha bathroom." I couldn't help but notice she had gotten a little thicker.


"Whew, I had to pee I was holding that for a while. Tex I know I've been grouchy and evil lately and I do apologize for that. I do want a commitment and I know I played hard to get in tha beginning but I just wanted to make sure it wasn't just about a piece of pussy."

"Mayla I could've gotten that from anybody."

"I know, that's why I needed to see if you really wanted me or to just get a shot of this snapper."

"Oh, that's what that is?"

"You know."

"You might have to refresh my memory."

"Sure will, after we finish talking. As I was saying, tha reason I've been cranky is because I'm pregnant."

"By me?" Tha look on my face must of said it all, "I mean I know by me but when? How far along are you?"

"Hawaii and 12 weeks."

"We went to Hawaii almost two months ago."

"And, how long have you known this?"

"About a month and a half."

"So why am I just finding out about it?"

"Because I was not sure if I was going to keep it or not."

"What?"

"Plus, you did say that you weren't ready for kids."

"Mayla that was over a year ago. Besides I never said I didn't want any I just said that at tha time I wasn't ready."

"Oh, so now you are?"

"Whether I am or not it doesn't matter because you'll be dropping' in 6 months."

"Tex I can raise this baby by myself."

"Now you talkin' stupid, what I look like not being in my child's life?"

"So, you want me to have it?"

"Would a poor man wanna become rich?" All I could do was smile when

Tex said that.

"I guess that explains your sudden mood swings."

"Damn!"

"What's wrong?"

"All y'all got knocked up in Hawaii."

"Yup, all except Paradise."

"That's some crazy Shit."

"Who you telling, our kids will be days apart."

"My son gon' be tha roughest."

"You don't know if it's going to be a boy or girl."

"Trust me, it's going to be a boy for sure."

"So, you want a junior?"

"That would be correct."

"Amillian Cortex Jr."

"We'll just call him Little Tex."

"Does this mean you're ready to stop playing tha field and settle down?"

"Yeah, I'm ready to start a family."

"Come wit me," she said walking up tha steps headed to tha bedroom.


"I don't know what it was but that was tha best sex we've had since we started messing."

"That's tha power of pregnant pussy."

"Oh yeah."

"Yeah, you know they say pregnant pussy is tha best."

"That's a myth, I had some that wasn't all that great."

"UNH, UNH, UNH, you a mess."

"Nah, I'm a man."

"How would you feel if another Nigga was knocking me down while I'm pregnant?"

"If I didn't know him I couldn't be mad at him. Now you on tha other hand I would kick a mud hole in ya ass."

"But you don't hit women."

"Shit for some disrespectful stuff like that it'll be tha first time."

"I would never disrespect myself or you like that."

"I don't have to worry about that because you know better.

"Ha! Ha! Ha!"

"You can laugh all you want but you heard what I said."

"Yes Daddy."

"Be funny all you want."

"Tex lets go shoppin' today."

"So you can hold me captive?"

"I was going to buy some maturity clothes today anyways. I thought you might want to go wit me."

"Fuck it, I'll go wit you if you really want me to."

"I wouldn't have asked you if I didn't."

"So, when is ya next doctor's appointment?"

"Monday morning."

"I'm going wit you."

"You don't have to."

"I know but I want to."

"Tex I would love for you to come."

"Mayla you tha Mother of my child and you'll probably be my wife one day."

"Now you sound like Jody from Baby Boy."

"Ha! Ha! Ha! That's where I got that from."

"Nah, but seriously you are my wifey now."

"Oh really?"

"Yes really, unless you object?"

"No not at all, I'm actually thrilled to be wifey."

"I'm bout to jump in tha shower."

"Can I join you?"

"I was hoping you would."

"Mayla I do want you to know that I will do right by you and our son."

"There you go wit that son shit again. What if it's a girl?"

"Then she'll be daddy's little diva, I won't love her any less. Maybe over protective but that's about it."

"Wow."

"Hey, I gotta make sure tha wolves don't try to get her."

"But ya son can be a player?"

"Hell yeah."

"Now you know that ain''t right."

"Why not?"

"Because you want him to do what you would not want done to ya daughter," when I didn't respond she said, "hello, don't get quiet now."

"Hey Man it is what it is."

"I hope we have a girl."

"When will they know tha sex?"

"I don't know, this is my first time too."

"At least I know why ya ass was getting fatter." She looked in tha full mirror.

"Do you think so?"

"Yes I do."

"I hope I don't get all big."

"I'm not going to let you."

"How you gon' stop me?"

"Easy, we gon' hit tha gym twice a week; that's how."

"Sounds good to me. Damn you really think my ass got fatter?" she asked making it shake like crazy.

"Now see what you did."

"Yup, let's get in tha shower, so you can bust my ass."

"You don't have to tell me twice."


After spending an hour in tha shower we decided to get out.

"I need to shoot to my crib to change my clothes."

"You got those outfits you bought hanging in my closet."

"Oh shit, I did put some clothes in there. I forgot all about them," I walked in tha closet and smiled when I saw tha Gucci jeans and V-neck shirt, "I can't go wrong wit this."

"Babe I put tha sneakers in tha back wit my shoes."

"Damn, I got sneakers too?"

"Tex you need to stop smoking so much weed."

"Yeah, I think you might be right. You do know that you won't be doin' no smoking or drinking?"

"Tex I stopped when I found out I was having a baby. But I am going out until I really start showing."

"I'm cool wit that, it's not like you go out every weekend anyway."

"As long as we on tha same page."

"Come on let's go."

"Where we going?"

"Jazz told me about this store in Cherry Hill that sells all name brand maternity clothes."

"A'ight."


As Tex was pulling off Jazz was calling my phone.

"Hello."

"Hey, did you tell him?"

"Yup."

"And what did he say?"

"We're on our way to that store you told me about in Cherry Hill."

"Bitch you was all worried about nothing."

"I know, and we even made our relationship official."

"Bitch no y'all didn't."

"Oh yes we did," I said looking over at my future husband who was all smiles.

"Put me on speaker."

"Why?"

"Just put me on speaker."

"Don't say nothing crazy."

"Tex."

"Yo."

"It took you long enough to make her happy."

"What's that 'pose to mean, I thought she was already happy?"

"She was but not as happy as she is now."

I looked at Mayla who was glowing. I couldn't front Mayla was bad as shit and she was about to have my child. All I could do was reach over and kiss her.

"Ooooh what was that for?"

"Just because I love you."

"Oh Shit, Mayla did he just say tha 'L' word." Mayla was speechless.

"Jazz Imma hit you back."

"Bitch don't pull over and try to get a quickie."

"Bitch bye."

"Tex we have been messing for over a year and you have never told me you LOVE me, not even when I tell you."

"I wanted to make sure, I don't take those three words lightly."

"And you shouldn't because I don't either. I didn't think you felt that way about me."

"As you know I've only been in love one time before."

"She broke ya heart but I won't."

"It took a lot for me to say those three words, but I meant them."

"Baby I love you too."

"Get that look off ya face I'm not pulling over, so we can Fuck."

"I didn't say pull over I can wait til we get to tha mall." Mayla spread her legs exposing her very clean-shaven vagina.

"See now you trying to tease me."

"No I'm not," she said dipping two fingers inside her.

"Here taste this," she said putting those same two fingers up to my mouth. I sucked those fingers like a lollipop.

"You so nasty."

"Looks whose talking Ms. Freaky Deaky."

"You love it."

"Yes, I sure do, every bit of it." As soon as we pulled into tha spot it was on.

# CHAPTER 22

## All Y'all Bitches Are Pregnant

"So all of you bitches are pregnant?"

"Yup and you might be too."

"I'm far from pregnant we never have unprecedented sex too bad y'all can't say tha same thing."

"We a'ight wit it."

"Do y'all have a choice?"

"We did but we chose to have our babies."

"How far along are y'all?"

"16 weeks."

"Damn y'all gonna have them kids days apart."

"I know right."

"I know Fourty and Stylz are a'ight wit it but what about Tex?"

"He loves it."

"Paradise you know they finally a couple."

"What? Bitch you should have been got knocked up."

"Same thing I said."

"He been pampering me so much."

"Awe Bitch stop complaining, you know you love it."

"Yes I do."

"Looks like I'll have three God children to spoil."

"They'll be calling you Aunty."

"They can call me what ever they want to call me, Imma still spoil them to death. What y'all want boys or girls?"

"I want a boy but Fourty wants a girl."

"We both want girls."

"When will they be able to tell tha sex?"

"Two more weeks."

"No more partying for y'all."

"I already told Tex I'm going out until I start showing."

"Well that won't be long."

"I mean really start showing."

"It's not like we really go out anyway."

"I know, only when it's a big party or special event."

"Speaking of special events there's a big party next week."

"Who's throwing it?"

"Tha boy from Wilmington."

"Oh, you talking about Cream."

"Yeah that's him."

"That nigga always wanna be in tha spot light."

"Word is he tha one that had Little Victor killed."

"Damn."

"Over a petty $10,000."

"Bitch you lying."

"No I'm not."

"If he had that boy killed for that chump change he's petty for real."

"$10,000 is a lot of money."

Jazz, Roxy, and Mayla all started to laugh.

"Let me in on tha joke."

"Bitch that ain't no lot of money Stylz just spent that on baby stuff."

"Well it's a lot of money for me."

"Shit you not going to have nobody killed for it especially if you suppose to be getting money like that."

"I see ya point."

"Maybe he ain't really gettin' money like he claim he is."

"Evidently not."

"Y'all know how niggaz make it look good."

"He definitely makes it look REAL good."

"To each its own."

"Tha funny thing is, he probably holding just not a lot compared to our men."

"I don't think nobody is getting money like them," said Paradise.

"After I have tha baby Tex is done wit tha game."

"Damn I hope Fourty feels tha same way."

"He probably does because Stylz said he's done too after tha baby is born."

"Yeah them niggaz holding if they just gettin' out in five months."

"When I first met Amir, he said he was done in a few years."

"They had a hell of a run."

"They'll probably turn it over to Buck and Twist."

"Them young bucks?"

"They been doing their thing this last year."

"What young boys?"

"Fourty nephews." I made sure to make a mental note just in case things didn't work out wit Amir.

"Bitch they too young for you."

"Stop disrespecting me Mayla." I saw tha wheels turning.

"Bitch I am not a cougar, them young boys can't do Shit wit or for me point blank."

"That's what ya mouth say."

"Yeah that's what it says and means."

"Anyway, y'all trying to go to tha party or not?"

"I'm game."

"Me too."

"I guess."

"Well it's settled, we can grab something to wear this weekend."

"Tex just took me shoppin' so I already got something to wear."

"Me too," said Jazz.

"I need something, so I'll go wit you Roxy."

"A'ight."

"Is there a theme?"

"I think it's an all-white affair."

"I got this bad all white Gucci pants suit."

"Giiiirl and I have this bad ass all white Dolce & Gabbana dress I knew it would come in handy."

"Is that tha dress you said Tex made you get?"

"Yup."

"So, he knew it would come in handy?"

"He just wanted me to get it because it showed of my beautiful curves as he put it. He said all tha niggaz mouths will be hanging on tha floor when I step into tha room."

"I swear if he don't sound like Fourty."

"Girl Stylz talks tha same way."

(THA PHONE RINGS) *There's Always That One Person Who Will Always Have Ya Heart.*

"That's my baby right there, hello."

"Hey Babe, you a'ight?"

"Yeah just talking to tha girls."

"Well tha boy Cream is having this all white party next weekend. Would you like to be my date?"

"We were just talking about that."

"So, you going wit them?"

"Baby I would love nothing more than to be ya date."

"We'll all end up going together anyway cause they going to ask them to go too."

"We going in a stretch Limo?"

"Nah, Imma pull tha Bugatti out."

"You do not have a Bugatti."

"Yes I do, I just don't drive it."

"What else don't I know about you?"

"Probably just as much as I don't know about you."

"Anyway."

"Just like I thought."

"Do you already have ya outfit?"

"Yeah, I just picked up my white Gucci linen I had made."

"Boy you just wanna dress like me."

"Babe I hate to be tha bearer of bad news, but ery body is going to be dressed like you."

"I'm not talking about tha white Mr. Smart Ass. I was talking about tha

Gucci."

"Well that's all I was calling about, I'll talk to you later."

"A'ight love you."

"Love you too."


"You over there making love."

"Bitch ain't nobody making love, I was talking to my man."

"What was he talking about that you had to go in tha corner to talk?"

"He just asked me to be his date next weekend to tha all white party."

"I guess we all got dates."

"Except me," said Paradise looking disappointed. Before she could say anything else her phone started ringing.

"Hello."

"Hey Ms. Paradise."

"Who is this?"

"Damn you don't know my voice by now?"

"Oh hey, I didn't recognize tha number."

"This my new number."

"OK I'll store it in."

"I was calling to see if you wanted to go wit me to tha all white party next weekend?"

"I would love to."

"Do you have something to wear?"

"No, me and Roxy are going to grab something this weekend."

"That's perfect, so are me and Stylz, so we can all go together. I thought you wasn't dealing wit me, you stop answering my calls."

"Amir I've fallen for you and I've fallen hard."

"Is that a bad thing?"

"Depends."

"Or what?"

"If tha feeling is mutual."

"Paradise you know you my baby."

"I can't tell you threw me on tha back burner for another bitch." Damn how she know that? I guess it's women's intuition.

"I didn't put you on tha back burner, you stop answering my calls remember."

"Are you going to keep throwing that in my face?"

"Not throwing it in ya face just stating tha facts."

"I can't win wit you Amir."

"How would you like to go to dinner tonight?"

"Sure, if you're treating."

"I wouldn't of ask if I wasn't."

"You always so defensive, I was only messing wit you."

"Yeah and so was I."

"Umm, Hmm I bet you was."

"You just be ready by 8 o'clock."

"That's right take charge."

"Always do, you should know that by now."

"Amir you something else, I'll be ready at 8 o'clock."


"Well, I guess you have a date now."

"Yup and a dinner date that I need to get ready for."

"What's wrong wit what you have on?"

"I wore this to work, I can't go to dinner wit this on."

"Girl you trippin'."

"You think I'm OK wit this on?"

"Yes, you're fine."

"A'ight then I'll keep this on. Let me call Amir and tell him to pick me up over here." I walked to tha kitchen to call Amir.


"She got it bad and don't even know it."

"She knows it, she just doesn't want to admit it."

"They been doing tha same song and dance for tha past 18 months."

"Hey, they cool wit what ever it is they doing so that's all it is."

"She wants more."

"How do you know that Mayla?"

"Trust me I know."

"You know what Mayla?" Paradise asked coming out of tha kitchen.

"That you want more from Amir than he's willing to give."

"How did you come up wit that assumption?"

"So, you telling me it's not true?"

"I plead tha fifth."

"Bitch you better tell him."

"I know that's right, give his is Ass an ultimatum."

"No don't do that, just be upfront wit him and tell him what you want."

"I was planning on doing that tonight anyway."

"Well it's about time."

"Fuck all y'all!"

"Are you going to tell him that you love him?"

"Why would I do that?"

"Because you do. Paradise y'all been talking for 18 months I know that you love him."

"Truth be told I do but I'm not going to tell him unless..."

"Unless what?"

"Unless he tells me, or I see some kind of indication that he does."

"You might be waiting a long time you know how men can be."

"Stylz told me he loved me before I told him."

"Well, ery body isn't like Stylz."

"I'm just saying it's possible he'll tell you."

"Possible yes likely no."

"Mayla shut up."

"I'm just being real, we talking about Amir."

"She has a point there, he has a good heart but he's not going to give it up like that."

"Has he been hurt in tha past?"

"Yup."

"That explains it."

"All you need to do Paradise is follow ya heart. If it says tell him, you love him then tell him; if it says don't tell him you then. Bottom line follow your heart."

"Shit, it's almost 8 o'clock let me go freshen up."

"Make sure you wash that cat."

"Bitch all you think about is sex."

"That's not all I think about, but I do love it."

"Don't we all," said Jazz rubbing her belly.

"Yes y'all do."

"You act like that's a bad thing."

"It's definitely not a bad thing especially if it's good."

"Bitch you need to get ya plumbing fixed."

"I plan on doing that tonight if things go according to plans."

"UNH, UNH, UNH, Bitch you something else."

"Runs in tha family but you already know that."

"It's almost 8 o'clock you better freshen up, you know Amir is always on time." As if on cue Amir was pulling up bumping Miguel's Adorn You.

"Paradise, Paradise, ya man just pulled up."

"Tell him I'm on my way out."

I just opened tha door and stuck my finger up indicating she was on her way out.

Damn Mayla was getting big as Hell. I was about to say something when Paradise walked out looking all good.


"Hello Amir."

"Good evening how are you?"

"I'm OK I hope I don't look all crazy."

"Nah, you straight."

"Oh, because these are my work clothes, I was gonna change."

"I'm glad you didn't."

"Now you trying to make me blush"

"Is it working?"

"Yup."

"Then I've done my job. What do you have a taste for Ms. Paradise?"

"I could go for some steak and shrimp."

"Have you ever had curry steak and shrimp before?"

"Shrimp but not steak."

"I know this spot in South Philly that has tha best curry steak and shrimp.

"Well let's go, turn me on to something new."

"Trust me you'll love it."


After 30 minutes we pulled to Shy's.

"Damn it's jampacked in there."

"It always is."

As soon as we walked in ery body starting greeting Amir like he was a celebrity. Even tha waiters knew him.

"Amir your usual table?"

"Yes please."

"OK follow me."

"I see you come here often."

"Yeah, at least once a week."

"You don't get tired of eating tha same food."

"No cause I always order something different."


"Hello Amir."

"Hey Cindy."

"What can I get for you for tha two of you?"

"I'll have tha curry shrimp teriyaki steak and shrimp wit tha garlic corn and potatoes."

"And you?"

"I'll have tha same but instead of tha corn can I please get tha broccoli?"

"Sure. What would y'all like to drink?"

"I'll take a bottle of Rozay."

"Umm I'll have a bottle too."

"We can share a bottle."

"Nah, I had a real hard day, so I need my own bottle."

"Hey suit ya self."

"Cin make it two bottles."

"A'ight I'll bring tha bottles right back."


"She likes you."

"Who Cin?"

"No Michelle Obama."

"That can't be possible we never met."

"You're such a smart ass, you know I'm talking about tha waitress."

"Cin is like a little sister to me."

"Yeah, I bet she is."

"My mom practically raised her."

"Boy I swear you got more games than tha Miami Heat."

"Here you go."

"Thanks."

"Hey mom called me today, she said she wants me to come over for dinner."

"She told me to come over Sunday for dinner too."

"Well, I'll see you Sunday."

"Of course you will."

"I'll bring ya food when it's ready."

"Don't be trying to rush off so you can talk to that nigga who keeps smiling at you."

"Who Javon?"

"I don't know his name."

"He's just a friend."

"As long as he treats you right I don't care what his name is."

"Stop being so overprotective."

"I'm just making sure my little sis is a'ight."

"You'll be tha first to know if I'm not."

"Speaking of, you haven't had any problems. out of Darnell, have you?"

"Hell no, he doesn't even look my way."

"Good."

"Well, let me check on tha food before I lose my job."

"I told you that you can run my real estate biz-ness."

"I'm still thinking about it."

"What is tha purpose of getting a degree in that field if you're not going to do that type of work? Hold on before you answer it's not a handout. I'll hold it on you tha same as I do all my other employees."

"No you won't."

"Try me and find out. I love you, but I won't let it interfere wit my biz-ness. Now go check on my food I'm starving."

"Wow."

"What?"

"You clearly love her."

"That's my little sister I never had."

"I think it's so cute tha way you play big brother tha protector."

"If I don't these niggaz will try to eat her alive."

"Amir I'm pretty sure she isn't a pushover."

"No but I still make sure she's always straight."

"I wish I had a brother like you."

"Trust me, no you don't."

"Yes I do."


"It's about time, I was about to complain to tha manager."

"So, you trying to get me fired?"

"If that's what it will take for you to work for me."

"Amir you know I love you to death, right?"

"Of course, I do Cindy."

"Listen, I'll call you in tha morning and we'll talk about it."

"Finally getting somewhere."

"Enjoy ya food, I need to get back to work."

"Make sure you do just that."

"What ever Big Head."

"Amir are you sure that's not ya blood sister?"

"Yes, I'm sure."

"Y'all favor one another and she acts like you cocky and arrogant."

"Ha! Ha! Ha! So, I'm cocky as well as arrogant huh?"

"Boy you know that you are so stop playing."

"Eat ya food before it turns cold."

"I guess that's your way of telling me to shut up."

"Nah, I just want you to be able to enjoy ya food while it's hot that's all."

"Umm, Umm, Umm, this steak is so delicious Damn."

"I tried to tell you." We made small talk as we both devoured our food.

"Amir let me ask you a question and I just want you to be honest wit me."

"No problem."

"How do you feel about me?"

"How do you feel about me?"

"You can't answer a question wit a question. But I will answer ya question, I've fallen in love wit you."

"I don't know if it's love but I do like you a lot and that's being really honest."

"I respect that."

"I'm glad you do."

"I know that most men have a hard time expressing themselves."

"I've been hurt in tha past, so it takes a lot for me to open up so don't take it personal."

"Thanks for waiting 18 months to tell me that."

"I'm sorry but I don't put my biz-ness out there like that."

"It's a'ight, somethings are too hurtful to rehash."

"You said that like you've been hurt in tha past also."

"I have, that's why I'm surprised that I feel this way about you. I'm even more surprised I let Mayla, Jazz, and Roxy Talk me into telling you how I feel."

"Oh, so you wasn't going to tell me how you felt about me?"

"Hell no."

"Wow, that was deep."

"I'm just keeping it real."

"I definitely respect ya honesty."

"If you don't mind me asking what happen; did you leave him?"

"No, he left me."

"Why?"

"He was killed in a home invasion."

"Sorry to hear that."

"It comes wit tha game."

"How long ago was this?"

"Three years ago."

"Hold on, tha only home invasion three years ago was my boy Chavez."

"You know Chavez?"

"Yeah he was my good people," I said not saying what I really wanted to say about him.

*Chavez was my man until tha Feds got in his head in turned him. He was trying to book me, but I was too smart for that Shit. Once I knew what he was doing I made it look like a home invasion and had him earthed.*

"Amir, Amir."

"Yo."

"Damn you lost in space."

"I was just thinking about Chavez. I'm still looking for those niggaz who did that shit. How long was your dealing wit Chavez?"

"Four years."

"A'ight enough about me, what about you?"

"She ran out wit a few dollars and some young boy."

"Now she's stupid."

"Some people let a few pennies blind them."

"How much is a few pennies?"

"$50,000."

"That's pennies to you?"

"Yup."

"I would love to see what you call money if 50K is pennies."

"500K or better."

"Amir you must be a millionaire."

"Put multi in front of that."

"I see tha game has been very generous to you over tha years."

"Most of my money comes legit through my biz-nesses."

I was starting to see Amir in a different light, he was more of a biz-nessman then he was a hustler.

"Amir, I thought you said you was going to retire from tha game?"

"I'm setting up for my exit now."

"Do you think you'll miss it?"

"No because truth be told I'm not that involved now."

"What about ya boys?"

"They about to be done too."

"That's what's up."

"Let me pay this tab so we can go."

"Make sure to leave ya sister a nice tip."

"Trust me I always do. This should cover it." Amir put about 15 100-dollar bills on tha table.

"Maybe I need to do a little waitressing tonight if you're tipping like that."

"Oh really?"

"Yes really."

"I know this sex shop where you can get a nice outfit from."

"I'm quite sure you do."

"Are you down?"

"Only if you dress up."

"Why do I have to dress up?"

"You're tha one who suggested it not me. If you scared say you scared." Little did she know me, and Liz did this all tha time.

"Cat got ya tongue."

"Paradise I'm far from scared."

"Well, take me to tha sex shop so I can make this a night for you to remember."

By tha time we left tha sex shop Amir had and outfit also.

# CHAPTER 23

## About Some Biz-ness

"Buck how's biz-ness been going?"

"Lonely."

"Are you ready to get out tha game yet?"

"Hell nah, I'm just getting started."

"That's what I wanted to hear."

"Why?"

"I'm about to retire and so is tha rest of tha squad."

"What do that have to do wit me?"

"We want you to take over."

"Hold up, are you saying that you going to introduce me to tha connect?"

"Yup."

"Unc it's really about to be on."

"Buck over tha past 18 months I've watched you grow from a boy to a man and that's why we all decided to give you as well as Twist tha reigns."

"Unc y'all were tha only ones standing in my way from running this Shit. And now that y'all giving me tha keys to tha city it's on!"

"Buck wit this there comes a lot more responsibility."

"I know, and I can handle it Unc."

"If we didn't think you could we wouldn't even be having this conversation."

"Are you busy now?"

"Nah, I was about to meet Twist on tha block."

"A'ight tell him to come here so we can go meet Stylz, Tex, and

Amir."


"Hello."

"Yo where you at?"

"On my way to meet you."

"Change of plans."

"What's up?"

"Meet me at Fourty's spot."

"Is everything a'ight?"

"I'll talk to you when you get here you know how I feel about phones." All I could do was smile at how smart Buck was.

"What you smiling at Unc?"

"I taught you well."

"All those times you thought I wasn't listening I was."

"So I see."


15 minutes later, Twist was pulling up wit Keesh in tha car.

"You don't mind if I ride wit you, do you?"

"Nah."

"A'ight Babe I'll hit you up later."

"OK," she said wit her lips puckered waiting for a kiss. Twist kissed her, and she went on her way.

"Nigga I don't know why you don't just buy Keesh her own car."

"I am for her birthday next month."

"Little Nigga don't try to buy her no squadder."

"Nah, she likes those 645 CI so Imma grab her a white one up."

"You know you got to give her tha works."

"Already on it."

"You two niggaz is learning."

"Hey, we have a good teacher."

"Yes you do," I said given myself props.

"Come on let's roll."

Twist looked at me as to ask what's tha deal. I hit him wit tha look that said just be patient. We pulled up to Ms. Tootsie's to be met by Stylz, Tex, and Amir.

"What's up fellas?"

"I can't call it Amir what's up wit you?"

"Same Shit just a different smell."

"Are we gonna stand here or go inside."

"Man just cause you all hungry don't be rushing us."

"Damn right I'm hungry I ain't ate all day."

"Mayla better start cooking for you."

"She does."

"Hey y'all."

"Hey Meek."

"Y'all need a table or is this to go?"

"We need a table please."

"Follow me."

"Sure will," said Twist looking at Meek's ass.

"Twist please, you scared of me."

"You don't really believe that ya self."

"Oh yes I do."

"Meek if I didn't mess wit Keesh I would've been gave you tha biz-
ness."

"All of tha sudden you're faithful?"

"Trying to be."

"Umm, huh, I'll be waiting on you."


"Damn Little Nigga she on you harder than a stripper on a pole."

"If I wasn't on my faithful shit trust me, she would've been knocked off
no questions asked."

"Well, if Fourty haven't told y'all we about to make an exit out of this
game."

"He told me a little bit."

"Well, I'm about to tell you a lot. After talking we all decided to let you
two take over."

"What? Are you Fuckin' serious?" Twist asked wit tha biggest smile on
his face.

"Of course we're serious."

"So, you telling me we gon' have tha plug?"

"Yup."

"Well, when do we start?"

"In a few months, and we'll introduce you to tha connect in three days.
Any questions?"

"All Imma say is we won't let y'all down and this will not go to our
heads."

"Yeah, just biz-ness as usual but on a higher scale. That's tha mind frame to have."

We talked, ate our food, and then Fourty dropped us off at my car.


"Damn Buck."

"What?"

"This is really happening."

"Hey this is what we wanted."

"Sure is Baby Boy."

"We gonna have to hire some guns to watch our back."

"For what? We are guns."

"True but better safe than sorry."

Yeah, you're right, I got two people in mind."

"Shots and Boom."

"How you know that's who I was thinking about? They're just as good as us if not better."

"As good as yes, better no."

"Let's go holla at 'em see if they want tha job."


"Well, Well, Well, what did you hear we did now?"

"Nothing, we need to holla at y'all about some biz-ness."

"Anything that got to do wit money we all ears."

"Listen, so big things are about to go down and we need some niggaz we can trust."

"You two Niggaz back on y'all Bullshit?"

"Nah, we on this money run tha city of Philly Shit."

"Hold up, are you going to war wit ya uncle and his team?"

"Hell nah."

"Then what's tha deal?"

"If you stop asking so many questions I'll tell you."

"Please tell," said Boom anxiously.

"My uncle is given us tha keys to tha city so we gon' be tha ones running this Shit in a few months."

"Oh OK, now I see y'all want us to have ya backs."

"Shit y'all been holding us down for a minute now it's our turn to return tha favor."

"Let me get ya number and I'll hit you in a few days."

"A'ight make sure you hit us up."

"We got y'all just stay outta trouble."

"Don't we always do?"

"Ha! Ha! Ha! Yeah right."


"Twist we'll be millionaires by tha time we reach 17."

"I'll be 17 in four months."

"I know when you'll be 17 Nigga."

"Damn what she want now?"

"Yo."

"Hey Babe."

"What up Keesh?"

"I'm about to do a little shopping wit Sash do you want me to bring ya car to you?"

"Where you at now?"

"At Sash house."

"Just leave tha keys at Bucks I'll have him swing me by to get them."

"OK love you."

"Love you too Baby Girl."

"Awe ain't that sweet."

"Tell Buck mind his biz-ness."

"Love you too Sis."

"What ever Big Head." Before I could say another word, my phone started to ring.

"Yes Sash."

"Don't say it like that."

"I'm not saying it like nothing feel bad I just knew you was going to call."

"I was just calling to say I love you."

"Ha! Ha! Ha!"

"What's so funny."

"You."

"Why am I funny."

"If you don't know neither do I."

"Boy what ever, I said I love you."

"Ditto."

"There you go wit that ditto Shit!"

"And there you go trying to prove a point to Keesh."

"No I'm not."

"Sash you told her if you told me you loved me I would say I love you too."

"Boy you know me to well."

"Yes I do."

"Sash."

"Yes Baby."

"I love you."

"Ha! Ha! Ha! I love you more."

"I doubt that."

"I don't."

"If I see something while I'm shoppin' I'll pick it up."

"You always do."

"I'll see you later."

"Do you want to go out for dinner tonight?"

"I took out some chicken."

"Just put it in tha fridge til tomorrow."

"Yeah because I know I'm not going to feel like cooking when I'm done anyway."

"A'ight call me when you done shoppin'."

"I've got a better idea why don't you come wit me and we go to dinner afterwards."

"OK I'm on my way."


"Yo I know you just didn't tell her you would go shoppin' wit her?"

"Yes I did, I'm not doing nothing else plus I could use some new clothes."

"Fuck now Imma have to go."

"Nigga you ain't gotta go."

"Nigga you know damn well Keesh gon' want me to go too."

"Spend some time wit ya wifey."

"Have you ever been wit Sash while she was shoppin'?"

"All tha time."

"How do you do it?"

"Easy, I help her pick what I know will look good on her."

"Man, I tried that."

"I don't know then it works for me."

"Shit if we're lucky they'll shop and let us shop."

"Hell nah!

"Why not?"

"Because we'll definitely be there all day."

"I learned that from Sash and my mom, trust me."

"Drop me off on tha block."

"Nah Nigga Imma take you to ya car after that it's on you."

"Yo you a sucka, you know damn well that ain't gonna fly."

"If you don't really want to go then you shouldn't have said you would."

"I don't mind going."

"That's because you always try to be stuck under Sash."

"Nah, I just like being around her and vice versa."

"Shit Nigga that's how you get tired of each other."

"Twist you still have a lot to learn when it comes to relationships."

"Buck, I know all I need to know trust me."

"Let me ask you something."

"Shoot."

"Would Keesh take a charge for you?"

"Of course, she would."

"Is she ya ride or die chick?"

"Yup."

"Is it safe to say she'll take a bullet for you?"

"Yup."

"So why wouldn't you want to spend a lot of time wit her?"

"That's just not me Buck."

"Believe me Twist it's not a bad thing."

"If it'll make you happy I'll go shopping wit y'all."

"Don't do it for me, do it because that's what you want to do."


"It took y'all long enough."

"I know, I was starting to think y'all changed ya minds."

"We should've."

"What you say Babe?"

"I said we're here and that's all that matters."

"You're right so let's go."

"And who's driving?"

"I'll drive," Sash said volunteering.

"We're going to King of Prussia."

"A'ight I need a new pair of Gucci sneakers anyway."


"Agent Sharp how close are you to closing this case?"

"I need a little more time Chief."

"Sharp over tha past six months you haven't given us anything to go on."

"I know but I'll have something soon."

"We're starting to think this thing has gone cold."

"No, not yet Chief."

"We're going to send Sheldon in wit you."

"No, he won't deal wit him."

"How do you know that?"

"Because he won't deal wit anybody he doesn't know."

"Well, maybe he should get to know him."

"Chief just trust me on this one."

"Sharp I do trust you, I just want to get this over wit, so we can both can get our promotions and lay back."

"Don't worry Chief that day is coming real soon trust me."

"I know, I know I'm just so anxious."

"So am I. All my hard work will pay off."

"Yes, it will Sharp yes it will."

"Chief I might be able to get one of his boys to deal wit Sheldon."

"Oh really?"

"Yeah, let me try to set it up and I'll get back wit you."

"A'ight."


I made sure to look around before exiting tha building. Once tha coast was clear I made my way to my car.

*I need to call and set up this appointment before I forget.* As soon as I hung up tha phone I made my way home to get some much-needed rest.


"Damn Girl you big as a house."

"Don't remind me Amir."

"How far along are you now?"

"Seven months."

"That's all?"

"Amir, I knew I had a bone to pick wit you."

"Awe stuff what I do now?"

"You gon' stop treating my cuzin' like that."

"Like what Mayla?"

"You know what I'm talkin' about so stop acting like you don't."

"Mayla I don't know what Paradise been telling you."

"She ain't have to tell me Shit I see it in her eyes."

"What do you see?"

"Pain, hurt, and love; do I need to continue?"

"Nah I get tha point."

"And don't tell her I'm saying this because she'll kill me if she knew."

"Me and P got an understanding."

"No Amir, you got a damn understanding she loves you a whole lot."

"That's my baby."

"Do you love her Amir?"

"That's my baby."

"That's not what I asked you."

"Well, I can't answer that."

"Why not?"

"Hey Mayla mind ya biz-ness."

"Paradise is my biz-ness she's blood."

"Evidently she doesn't care, you fighting more than her."

"Tex why you always got something to say?"

"Same reason you always in Paradise's biz-ness."

"Don't even say it."

"You get on my nerves," I said at tha same time she did.

"I'm on my way to tha grocery store."

"Can you grab me some fruit please?"

"Only because you said please."

"You must be making some of tha fruit cocktail?"

"And you know it."

"Damn I can't wait to have this baby."

"I'll make you a virgin cocktail like always do."

"Fuck a virgin, I want tha real deal."

"Baby you got tha real deal."

"Ha! Ha! Ha! You so conceited."

"I know."

"What do you want for dinner?"

"You."

"Boy you can't get enough of me I see."

"You won't get an argument outta me on that one."

"Ha! Ha! Ha! I bet she won't."

"Don't cosign that Shit Amir."

"I'm just speaking I'm not cosigning Shit." Mayla just looked at me wit a smile.

"But seriously Amir, Paradise really loves you."

"Matter fact. let me call her and see what she's up to."

# CHAPTER 24

## Our Baby Showers

Shit it seems like as soon as I went to sleep my phone started to ring.

"Hello."

"Hey Roxy."

"Oh, hey Jazz."

"Was you sleep?"

"Trying to."

"Well I'll call you back."

"No you good, my phone not going to let me get no sleep anyway."

"Well, I was thinking that we should rent a hall and tha three of us have our baby showers together."

"Mayla said tha same thing yesterday."

"It just makes sense instead of three separate ones."

"Mayla is going to find a hall."

"We can have it at tha Embassy in tha ballroom."

"Giiirl you know tha waiting list for that is at least a year."

"Yeah but not when Uncle Darrell runs it."

"Oh Shit, I forgot about Uncle Darrell running that."

"Yeah and I already talk to him about it, all I need to know is what day do we want it for?"

"Hold on let me call Mayla on tha three-way."


"Hello."

"Hey, remember we was talking about tha baby showers?"

"Yeah."

"Well, what about tha Embassy?"

"Bitch you know damn well tha waiting list is at least a year."

"Not when ya uncle runs it."

"Who's that, Jazz?"

"Yeah."

"Hey Bitch."

"I'm a damn good one too."

"I bet you are."

"Anyway, what day do y'all want it on?"

"How about tha Saturday after next? That way it will give us all time to send out invitations."

"Sounds good to me."

"Me too."

"Well, that's all it is then I'll let my uncle know."

"What time?"

"4 PM to 9 PM."

"What about tha food?"

"I'll have my aunt cook."

"Oh yeah, Ms. Betty can definitely burn. She's gonna need some help cooking all that food."

"My aunts and Nana will probably help her. So if y'all have something pacific that y'all want let me know and I'll pass it on."

"All I want is some of that banging seafood pasta Nana makes."

"Roxy she's gonna make that anyway."

"Well, what about her famous shrimp crab cakes?"

"Bitch I'm already on that. What about you Jazz?"

"Tell me what's already on tha menu."

"Chicken, meatballs, seafood pasta, shrimp crab cakes, shrimp, mac & cheese, collard greens, and a whole bunch more."

"Only thing I could think of is stuffed green peppers."

"Bitch what you know about that?"

"Come on what Black person doesn't?"

"I'm bout to fix me something to eat y'all got a bitch hungry now."

"No ya ass just Fuckin' greedy."

"That's Lil Stylz."

"If you keep that up you're not going to be able to lose tha weight afterword's."

"Look who's talkin'."

"Yeah, but tha differences is I work out 3 or 4 times a week and you don't."

"Bitch you don't know what I do."

"I know you don't work out."

"How do you know that?"

"Let me see, could it be that Stylz is always asking me to take you to tha gym wit me."

"Imma cuss him out for that bullshit."

"How are you gon' be mad at him for trying to help you out."

"You always taking up for him."

"That's my brother."

"What ever and for tha record I do work out."

"Y'all are crazy."

"No Mayla is crazy."

"How do y'all want to do tha invitations?"

"Put all our names on it since we have tha same friends."

"Yeah because it won't make sense to do three separate ones."

"I'll do tha invitations I have something special I want to do."

"Fine you got that."

"I'll do one then let y'all see it."

"Just do them all."

"How many do you think I should make?"

"Just make a hundred that should be more than enough."

"A'ight I talk to y'all later."

"OK."

"Imma call my aunt and Nana."


"This little boy is very active I know that."

"Is he kickin' again?"

"Feels more like stompin'."

"He's ready to enter tha world."

"Well, he has two more months before that happens."

"He's just like his daddy."

"What's that?"

"Impatient."

"It never stops wit you."

"I learned it from you."

"Sure you did."

"Me, Jazz, and Roxy decided to have our baby showers together."

"That makes a lot of sense."

"We figured we all know tha same people so why not knock out three birds wit one stone."

"That must be a big ass stone."

"Boy shut up," she said punching me in tha arm.

"Well, I don't think Lil Tex needs anything except pampers and maybe bibs."

"Yeah because you got him everything else."

"Hey, it's my first child gotta make sure he strapped like a suicidal bomber."

"Boy you stupid shut up."

"Where are y'all having it at?"

"Tha Embassy."

"Damn, how y'all pull that off?"

"Roxy and Jazz uncle runs it."

"Helps to know people."

"Yup sure does."

"Let's go get some lunch."

"Sounds good we hungry."

"When aren't you?"

"My aunt and Nana will be cooking tha food."

"Seriously?"

"Yeah."

"I know that baby showers are for women, but I might have to come for some of that food."

"They're not just for women most men just don't want to come."

"Matter fact, you can just bring me a big fat plate wit a little of everything on it."

"Yeah a'ight."

"You wouldn't do that for me ya future husband slash baby dad."

"Absolutely not."

"I would do it for you if tha roles were reversed."

"But they're not so."

"So what?"

"Either you gon' come or you not getting no plate."

"Babe if you want me to come all you have to do is ask."

"Tex will you please come to my baby shower?"

"I need to see if Stylz and Fourty are going first."

"No you don't."

"Yes I do, I'm not going to be tha only dude there."

"Why not, you like to be tha center of attention. Let me find out you scared."

"Like Bone Krusher said I ain't never scared."

"That's what ya mouth says."

"How long have we been together?"

"Almost two years."

"Wow, I guess you don't know me at all then."

"Oh, I know ya spoiled ass."

"Really."

"Yes really."

"Come on let's go."

"What do you have a taste for?"

"Ya son is craving Chinese."

"Well Ms. Won's is tha closest."

"I don't like her food that much."

"Me either."

"Then why would you suggest it?"

"I wanted to see what you were gon' say."

"How about Chung Li's then?"

"Now we talking, all you can eat buffet?"

"Look at you don't make no sense all greedy."

"Not me him," she said pointing to her stomach.

"It's a good thing I keep you in tha gym."

"Boy pleeeease, l go cause I don't want to be all fat and outta shape."

Tex starts singing, *"I'll Still Love You If You Gain A Little Weight Just as Long as Ya Love Don't Change."*

"OK, OK Musiq Soulchild"

"Hey Man, I try."

"Sounds like you got vocals."

"I do OK."

"Hmm."

"Told you you don't know me."

"Tex I knew you sing I heard you in tha shower."

"No you didn't," I pulled out my phone found what I was looking for then pressed play, "oh Shit! Wow I sound good."

"So damn conceited."

"I'll take that as a compliment coming from you."

"Well say thank you."

"Thank you, Mrs. Cortex."

"Oooh I like tha sound good."

"I'm sure you do, play ya cards right and it will be reality."

"Play my cards right?"

"Before you start I'm just playing Baby."

"About what? Me being Mrs. Cortex?"

"No playing ya cards right."


When we pulled up to Chung Li's it was a little crowded.

"Damn, I see we weren't tha only ones wanting Chinese."

"I guess not."

We were shown to our seats. Mayla let tha waiter know that we wanted tha buffet before he could hand us our menus. He told us to help ourselves.

"Baby look at all this new stuff they added since tha last time we were here."

"I know, Imma try this shrimp crab roll it looks good." Once we had what we wanted we made it back to our table."

"This shit is banging."

"We gon' have to see if we can get a box to go."

"As long as we pay I'm pretty sure it won't be a problem."


"Is everything OK?"

"Do you think I can pay for a box to go?"

"Yes, but we weigh for you then you pay."

"No problem, matter of fact bring two boxes please."

"OK I'll be right back."

"Take ya time we still eating anyway."

"Umm, Umm, Umm, this is good."

"Aren't you glad I wanted Chinese?"

"Yes, I'm glad y'all wanted Chinese."

"Tex have I told you how much I love you today?"

"No you haven't."

"Well, I love you deeply."

"Ditto."

"Hey Mayla."

"Yes."

"You had me chasing you for damn near a year."

"Tex I thought you just wanted some pussy."

"I did but I wanted you too."

"I figured if you would chase me for that long then it wasn't about tha pussy."

"So, you didn't want me?"

"Hell yeah, but I wasn't just going to give in so easy to you."

"Yo you crazy."

"That's what Roxy and Paradise said too."

"Well, it was worth tha wait and tha chase."

"Yes it was, yes it was."

Tex starts singing again, *So Ya Having My Baby, and It Means So Much to Me.*

"Now you Jodeci?"

"Nah. I just like tha song."

After we boxed our food up we paid and then left.

"Whew, I'm stuffed."

"Me too, I'm ready to lay down now."

"You took tha words right out of my mouth."

"Tex ya phone ain't gon' let you get no sleep."

"Shit I'm turning this Mafucka off for tha rest of tha day and night."

"Oooh so that means you staying in wit me?"

"Yup unless you don't want me to."

"Boy stop playing, I would love for you to stay and cuddle wit me."

"I'm all yours."

"Do you think it's possible for me to get my thing off."

"My son has you so horny all tha time."

"I thought you liked it."

"Nah Baby I love it."

"I got this bomb ass pussy and you love it."

"I'm not denying that."

"Well hurry up home so you can get ya self some bomb pussy and head."

I stepped on tha gas and got us home in 15 minutes.

# CHAPTER 25

## I Was Real Busy wit this Case

"I need a little more time."

"You need a little more time for what?" I must of startled her because she jumped when I asked her that.

"Boy don't be sneaking up on me like that."

"I didn't sneak I walked right up."

"You were just so into ya phone conversations that you didn't hear or see me."

"That was work this civil case I'm working on has me swamped."

"That explains why I haven't seen you much as of late."

"Yup been tied up."

"I bet you have been."

"Not like that smart ass."

"Are ya fingers broke?"

"You too damn smart."

"Are they?"

"No."

"So why didn't you pick up tha phone and call me?"

"I just told you I was busy."

"All night too?"

"No."

"That's what I thought. Ya mouth and ya actions are saying something else."

"Amir how I told you I feel about you is tha truth."

"You sure?"

"Yes I am, I've just been real busy wit this case."

"That must be a real important case that you don't have time for me tha person you claim to have fallen in love wit."

"Amir don't do that!"

"Don't do what, tell it like I see it?"

"Hey if that's tha way you feel you're entitled to feel like that."

"This is just me but if I confess my love for person Imma make sure I see and talk to them as often as possible, but that's just me."

"Well, I'm sorry you feel that way trust that was not my intention at all."

"It's cool P."

"Wow P now?"

"My bad, it's cool Paradise."

"You had to be spoiled coming up."

"Not really."

"So, you trying to tell me that your parents didn't spoil you?"

"Yup my pops got killed in a home invasion and my mom overdosed on heroin."

"Well, I thought you and Cindy just had dinner wit ya mom."

"I'll show you a picture of my mom next time you come to my spot."

"That'll be soon."

"If you say so and I call my Nana mom, she raised me since I was six years old."

"Ya pop-pop that left you ya money is that ya Nana's husband?"

"Yes."

"Are you staying wit me tonight or do you need to get home?"

"Would you like me to stay wit you tonight?"

"If you don't mind."

"Then I guess I'll be staying wit you tonight."

"I hope you're not tired because I need to get my thing off badly."

"Paradise if you take time out and stop overworking yourself then you wouldn't be so backed up."

"I know, now you sound like Mayla."

"Mayla is my peeps and she is all team Amir and Paradise."

"Trust me Amir I know that."

"I respect that not too many people would do tha things for family that she does."

"She is going to make a good mother."

"Man, that little boy is going to be spoiled rotten."

"Between them and us."

"Paradise, I got three nephews on tha way."

"Amir what was tha chances of them all getting pregnant at tha same time then all of them having boys?"

"Hey all I can say was it was meant to be."

"Did you get and invitation to tha baby shower next week?"

"Yeah."

"Are you going?"

"Ain't that shit for women?"

"No."

"Then I'll probably go, I have to do a little shopping for my gifts."

"They said all they need is bibs and stuff like that."

"Man, I ain't showing up wit no damn bibs!"

"Imma get them some clothes and sneaks."

"That's what I was thinking too."

"They not going to need no gear until they get at least one years old."

"We might as well go together, I know this store up New York that has all that fly name brand shit for babies and kids."

"So, you telling me Imma need to bring $20,000?"

"Whoa, Whoa, Whoa I didn't say you need all that."

"Oh, you don't know how I shop, that's chump change."

"To you maybe."

"Paradise three kids about 6 to 7 grand a piece, shit you right Imma need more than that."

"Why don't you just bring $50,000?" I said only joking wit him.

"You know what, you're right because Imma buy myself some things too."

"Amir, Imma jump in tha shower you're more than welcome to join me."

"Why don't you take a nice milk bath that will help you to relax."

"I think that's exactly what I need a milk bath and some good sex."

"Trust me you're going to get both."

"Umm, Umm, that sounds like a definite winner."


By tha time I got out tha tub Amir was laying across tha bed smoking a Dutch.

"Can I have some of that?"

"Sure," he said passing me tha Dutch.

"I didn't know you smoked."

"Not all tha time like you but I do."

"Well you better take ya time wit that it's some exotic."

"I can handle it jus like I handle you."

"Hmm well see about that, lay across tha bed so I can give you a rub down."

"You ain't gotta tell me twice. Oooh yup that feels soooo gooood!"

"These hands are magic."

"Sure feels like it."

I rubbed Paradise down from her head to her feet making sure to hit every spot, even ones she didn't know existed.

"Damn Amir, those hands just might be magic."

"Baby this is just tha beginning we have all night."

Hearing Amir say that had my pussy moist. I turned over so that he could do tha front just like he done tha back.

"Do you mind if I take my towel off?"

"Shit I was hoping you did." Once tha towel was off I started to rub her shoulders and her breast.

"Ooooh, Umm, that feels good."

As I worked my way down to her stomach I could see her arch her back. When I started rubbing her inner thighs Paradise really started to gyrate her hips.

"AAAAH SHIT AMIR!"

Tha icing on tha cake was when I put one of her nipples in my mouth. I slowly worked my way down to her stomach then to her vagina. She tried to hold her composure but once I sucked on that little man in tha boat she lost it.

"OOOOH YES RIGHT THERE DADDY. OH MY GOD DON'T

STOP AMIR!"

I knew what had her right where I wanted her at. While taking my thumb and index finger I caressed that little man while blowing in her vagina which really set her into a frenzy.

"SHIT! SHIT! SHIT! DAMN I'M CUMIN'!!!"

As soon as her body started shaking like a stripper I sucked on that little man so hard it made her have multiple orgasms that even she couldn't control. When I felt she was just about to stop I slid in her nice and slow causing her to really have a long hard orgasm.

"FUUUCK!"

I have never had orgasms like this before not even wit Amir. I don't know what he was trying to do to me, but I was officially whipped and in love wit him. He continued to sex me like crazy for tha remainder of tha night until we both fell asleep.

Tha next morning when I woke up Amir was gone but there was a note on tha nightstand.

> *Paradise,*
>
> *Sorry I couldn't wake you up to a nice orgasm, but I had an important meeting. There's a plate for you in tha microwave enjoy it.*
>
> *Amir*

This boy probably went to McDonald's and got me something to eat; hey it's tha thought that counts. After washing my face and brushing my teeth I made my way to tha kitchen. Talk about surprise, boy I was surprised to open tha microwave to a plate of fried potatoes, beef bacon, scrambled eggs, and strawberry waffles. I wonder where he bought this from, it sure looks good. I set tha timer for three minutes and waited Damn it sure smells good. I'm not gonna front I tore that plate up. I need to call him to see where he got this from. After four rings he picked up.

"Were you busy?"

"No, just finishing up wit my meeting, why what's up?"

"Where did you buy that food from?"

"Ha! Ha! Ha!"

"What's so funny Amir?"

"Why did I have to buy it why couldn't I have cooked it myself?"

"Because I know you didn't cook that."

"That's another of my hidden talents."

"So, you trying to tell me you made that?"

"Yes, I left tha rest of tha stuff in ya fridge."

I opened tha fridge and sure enough tha stuff was in there. I put tha waffles in tha freezer.

"Damn Boy if you can cook breakfast like that I can only imagine what dinner taste like."

"There's only one way to find out."

"So, you plan on cooking for me one night?"

"Not one night tonight."

"Wow, I feel honored."

"You should, I've only cooked for one other lady."

"Wow."

"What do you have tha taste or craving for?"

"Question is, what can you cook?"

"What ever you want."

"Just surprise me then."

"I'll see you around 7:30 PM."

"I'll definitely be here."

"A'ight see you then."

"Bye."

"Damn, let me call Mayla."


"Hello."

"Bitch guess what."

"What?"

"Not only did Amir stay tha night and sex me like no other but he made me this banging breakfast."

"Bitch stop lying!"

"I am not lying and he's making dinner later for us."

"You must of finally gave him some head."

"Bitch he been got tha head."

"Damn you so sneaky."

"No I'm not. Mayla I reeeeallly love him."

"Yeah but does he feel tha same way about you?"

"Honestly, I don't know Cuz."

"Well, find out before you get ya heart broke."

"Mayla I'm going to ask him point-blank tonight if there's a chance for us."

"What if he says no? Because you know that he does have a girl."

"He told me that when we first started talking. If there's not a chance I'm a cut my losses and move on."

"Yeah right, not tha way you just said you was all in love."

"True but what sense does it make to keep wanting somebody that will never belong to you?"

"That's a question only you can answer for yourself."

"Mayla I'll talk to you later."

"A'ight hit me and let me know how it all works out."

After I hung up I called tha office to let them know that I wouldn't be in today for my own personal reasons. Since it was only 10 o'clock I had about nine hours before Amir would be back to cook dinner then beat this pussy up all over again. Just tha thought of that got my pussy moist so I decided to get in tha shower and please myself. Once I was done, I got dressed then headed to South Street to do a little shoppin'.


"Paradise is that you?" I turned around to see Roxy and Stylz.

"Hey y'all"

"Ooh somebody Is playing hooky today."

"Yeah, I needed some me time."

"Bitch I know how that is."

"Oh do you?" Stylz asked.

"Yup tha way you pluck my nerves."

"Ha! Ha! Ha! Roxy you trippin'."

"That's what you want me to think."

"I think you're tha one plucking somebody's nerves."

"You two are something else."

"That's her Paradise, ever since she got pregnant she's been a piece of work."

"Well Stylz, it's a good thing you only have a couple more months to deal wit it then."

"This little nigga ain't coming fast enough."

"All you gon' do is spoil him anyway."

"Sure ya right."

"Well let me do a little shoppin' Roxy I'll talk to you later."

"A'ight Paradise."

(PHONE RINGS) "MY NIGGAZ SOME NIGGAZ THAT YOU DON'T WANNA TRY, MY NIGGAZ SOME NIGGAZ THAT BE READY TO DIE."

"What up Amir?" At tha sound of his name I sparked up another conversation wit Roxy.

"Look at you, heard Amir's name and tha world stops."

"Bitch that's my baby even though I'm not his."

"How do you know that?"

"You know ya girl right here."

"Hold on." Stylz went to give me his phone but I didn't take it.

"Tell him he knows my number." Hi, listened as he passed tha message on.

"A'ight I'll tell her," he said then flipped his phone shut.

"Tell me what I know."

"He said something smart."

"All he said was just be where you need to be at 7 o'clock."

"Umm somebody getting some tonight."

"Bitch shut up!"

"Ha! Ha! Ha! I'll talk to you later."

"No, you'll probably talk to me tomorrow."

"Bye Bitch!"

"Bye Stylz."

All I could do was laugh on my way down tha street because Roxy was right. I planned on having a blazing dinner then getting dicked down to sleep. How in tha Hell did I let myself fall for Amir like this? He seriously had me whipped like cream. Damn I love me some Amir. I stopped in Unica for Kids to see if they had something for tha boys. By tha time I finished shoppin' it was 5:30 so I made my way home.

# CHAPTER 26

## Who Can We Really Trust

"Listen we called this meeting because there are about to be some serious changes and we need to know who we can really trust."

"You can trust me."

"Yeah me too, I'm wit y'all no matter what; here's a few of tha responses we got."

"Good, Good, Good that's what I wanted to hear because each of you in here will be running ya own crew, so I really suggest you get some people you can trust as we do y'all."

"What are you two niggaz up to?"

"We wanted to see who we could really trust."

"Listen, we bout to kill tha plug and take 100 bricks."

"Hold on ain't ya uncle and his boys tha plug?"

"Yeah."

"You gon' off ya uncle?"

"Damn right for 100 chickens. Are you niggaz down or what?"

"Imma keep it real, I don't agree wit it but you my dog so Imma rock all tha way out wit you."

"Buck you know we gon' have to off tha whole squad."

"I know."

"Ha! Ha! Ha! Man, I'm not killing my uncle or his squad I just wanted to make sure you niggaz was really down to ride."

"Thank God but I was gon' ride wit you."

"I see."

"So we ain't really gettin' our own crew?"

"Nah, that part is real, my uncle and them turning tha city over to us in about another month."

"Word."

"Yeah word."

"It's really about to be tha Fuck on."

"I say that's right, everything in Philly comes thru us."

"We from tha home of Philly where we cook out every day."

"A little young gunz in ya life?"

"Yeah Man."

"Ain't nothing wrong wit it them my peeps."

"So, we about to run tha city of Philly?"

"Yeah, we bout to have tha city in tha palm of our hands."


(KNOCK, KNOCK, KNOCK)

"Come in."

As soon as Boom and Shots walked in ery body went for their pistols.

"Whoa, Whoa, no need for that, we on tha same team."

"Y'all can relax, we called them here."

Ery body in tha room knew that Shots and Boom where killers and wouldn't hesitate to pull tha trigger. I remember when we first met them.

"Hey Buck, you ready?"

"Sho nuff."

"A'ight make sure ya mask is pulled down tight."

"Y'all Mafuckas know what it is."

"That's right run that Shit." Boom and Shots were already sticking tha spot up, but we didn't care.

"Drop ya guns, don't try nothing stupid because we will send you Niggaz straight to tha boneyard."

Bone looked at Shots who nodded his head. They knew from tha seriousness of their voice they would kill them if they tried something. Boom and Shots were our old heads that we respected because of tha work we heard they put in, but they are in tha wrong place tonight. Once we had all tha money I made old man Travis take me to tha safe he had in tha back that he thought nobody knew about.

"What safe?"

"Do we have to play this game Old Man?"

"I don't know..."

(POP!)

"AAH SHIT!"

"Next time it won't be a leg shot. Now are you going to open tha safe or not?"

"Yeah sure, what ever you want just don't shoot me again."

After I emptied all tha contents of tha safe I signaled for Twist and we rolled out. After tallying up tha take we ended up wit close to a quarter of mill. We both out of respect for Boom and Shots decided to hit them $50,000 to split.

"Boom, Shots."

"Yeah who you?" Boom asked reaching.

"Hold on Big Man before this thing gets out of hand."

"Who tha Fuck are you? Did ya dad send you?"

"Ha! Ha! Ha! Nah, I came to give you this."

"Hold on easy Cowboy."

I reached under my shirt then handed him tha bag and when he looked inside he handed it to Shots.

"So, who do you want dead?"

"Old Head I put my own work in, this is for tha other night at tha Crap Spot."

"Oh Shit, that was you?"

"Yeah, we didn't know y'all were already in there. It was too late once we were in. This is just out of respect."

"Damn how old are y'all?"

"13."

"Damn Boom I like these little two niggaz."

"Me too, I definitely have a lot of respect for y'all. Not too many people who have done this," he said holding tha bag of money, "shit nobody would've done that I know I wouldn't have."

"My uncle said always respect ya elders."

"Ya uncle's a smart man."

"Ever since then they've been our old heads since."


"Listen Boom and Shots are wit us, I just wanted them here to know what's going on."

"Don't worry you little niggaz had a pass anyway on tha strength of Buck and Twist. We have a lot of love for those two niggaz, so we would never cross them."

"We're just glad you're on our side."

"Young Buck trust me if we weren't you would have been known." We put ery body on tha same page of what we expected.

"If nobody has anything else then we can roll."


"Sharp tell me something good."

"Chief I'm still at tha same spot."

"Do you think he's on to you?"

"No, he's just not that involved in tha game so it's hard to catch him wit his hand in tha cookie jar."

"Well, I hope you can come up wit something real soon. Chief I think we need to squeeze one of tha smaller guys to get them to rollover."

"At this point, anything is worth a try."

"I'll make it happen in tha next few days."

"Fair enough."

"Chief, are your superiors putting tha pressure on you?"

"No, they told me to let you handle it your way."

"So why are you putting a rush on me?"

"Sharp I don't want him to slip away this time this is tha closest we've ever been to bringing him down.

"Chief, you have to have a little more patience."

"I know, I know, I just want this scum bag so badly."

"So do I chief."

"But I know if I don't take my time that something can go wrong."

"I agree and I'm sorry just take your time. I'll still bring one of tha smaller guys in to see what we can squeeze out of him."

"Do you think that is wise?"

"I won't do tha interview."

"OK."

"Just make sure it's one of those punks that will talk."

*Facing enough time, I think all tha low in hustlers will talk, so I thought anyway.*

We ended up bringing four guys in but none of them would talk. I had to admit these guys had a lot of respect for Amir he must be treating them right.

# CHAPTER 27

## Tanya Montana

"Hey Amir."

"What up Smoke?"

"You know tha alphabet boys grabbed me up."

"Oh yeah when?

"Yesterday."

"Was you dirty?"

"No, they kept asking a lot of questions about you."

"Me?

"Yeah, you and tha fellas."

"What did you tell them?"

"Come on, Amir I don't get down like that I'm loyal you should already know that."

"Hey, you be surprised what that pressure will do."

"Yeah to a weak Mafucka not a real nigga. Amir some niggaz want to play tha game but can't handle tha consequences that come wit tha game. You need to watch ya self."

"Smoke I'm done wit this Shit, I'm just tying up some loose ends."

"Why you ain't let a nigga know?"

"Because you'll be straight, Buck and Twist will be taking over, and I already told them to make sure you straight."

"A'ight bet."

"Imma holla at you later Little Homey."

"Cool."

"Thanks for tha heads up."

"No-brainer you my old head."

"I'm far from old."

"I heard that." (BEEP-BEEP)

"Damn Amir who's that?"

"Oh, that's my baby right there."

"She bad, she got any sisters?"

"Yeah but she's old enough to be your mom."

"I love a cougar."

"Ha! Ha! Ha!"

"Hey Babe."

"Hey, what you laughing at?"

"My young boy, he asked me if you had sisters."

"Joanne can be his mom."

"I told him he said he loves a cougar."

"He wouldn't know what to do wit her."

"Hey never judge a book by its cover Liz."

"I know that's right," she said licking her lips at me.

"You better stop before I end up on top of you in this truck."

"Mmm, that doesn't sound like a bad idea I haven't been fucked in a car in decades."

"You are a real freak Babe."

"Only for you Amir."

"Tha average joker wouldn't know what to do wit you."

"Don't I know it."

"Them old dudes couldn't keep up wit you Babe."

"Right again."

"Let me stop blowing ya head up."

"Baby you not telling me nothing I don't already know."

"Must you be so Damn conceited?"

"I've been around you too long."

"Oh, is that what it is?"

"I believe so."

"Dammit ain't nowhere to park."

"There's a spot right there." We parked and then walked into tha restaurant.


"Hello, my name is Heidi table for two?"

"Yes please."

"Follow me please. Is this table OK for you?"

"Yes, it's fine Heidi."

"What would you like to drink while you look over your menu?"

"I'll have a bottle of Rozay."

"Just water for me."

"A'ight I'll let your waiter know." Ten minutes later, Camron our waiter came wit our drinks and menus.

"I'll give you some time to look over tha menu and come back."

"Damn he should just ask you your name as hard as he was staring."

"He not thinking about me."

"Yeah right."

"Do I detect a little jealousy?"

"Nah because if I wasn't wit you I'd be looking too, I wouldn't be as noticeable though."

"Thanks for tha compliment."

"My pleasure, you don't want any of this?"

"No I can't."

"Why not?"

"Well because I just found out I'm pregnant."

"Huh?"

"Yup, just found out today."

"So that's what you had to talk to me about?"

"Yes, truth be told I didn't think I could have kids."

"So, what do you want to do?"

"That's what I was going to ask you."

"Liz, I'm 23 wit no kids."

"I kind of figured you probably wouldn't want to have any kids."

"Are you going to let me finish before you start assuming?"

"I'm sorry, finish what you were saying."

"I'm 23 wit no kids so I would love to have a child."

"Whew, I was hoping you did because I was going to have my baby regardless."

"How far along are you?"

"Ten weeks. You can tell ya other bitches they don't have to worry about no baby mama drama from me."

"That's tha least of my concerns or worries. I know you ain't petty plus by tha time little lady is born there will be no other bitches as you say."

"Oh, so you want a girl?"

"Yup, so I can spoil her to death."

"Well, I want a son."

"How far long do you have to be to know tha sex?"

"I think it's four months or better."

"When is your next appointment?"

"Two weeks."

"I'm going wit you."

"No problem, I would love for you to go wit me."

"I'll be going to all your appointments from this point on."

"You don't have to do that I can get Joanne to go or just go by myself."

"How that sound me letting you my baby mother go to tha doctors by herself."

"I'm just saying I know you be busy that's all."

"Not too busy for that plus I'm done wit tha game."

"Done wit tha game since when?"

"Well actually, I've been transitioning out for tha past few weeks."

"So Tex and tha boys are taking over?"

"Nah they all done too."

"Damn tha city is gonna be all jacked up."

"They'll be a'ight, Buck and Twist will be holding it down."

"Evidently they are capable if you're putting tha city in their hands."

"Liz, I remember when those two were so reckless, they came a long way."

"Ok they came a long way, but do they have what it takes to run Philly?"

"I believe so."

*Since he decided to walk away from tha game maybe he'll have more time for me.*

"What's on ya mind?"

"Nothing just thinking."

"About?"

"Just about how I won't have to worry if my child's father will be alive or free."

"Baby I'll be both even if was still in tha game."

"What made you leave tha game alone?"

"I told myself I was in and out in 10 years no matter what I got; it just so happens I've got a lot out of tha game."

"Baby you have four successful biz-nesses and probably worth a lot of money so that says a lot."

"Truth be told, Joanne told me that tha store is really yours."

"Amir, I was heavy in tha game some years back."

"Do you know that chick they called Tanya Montana?"

"What about her?"

"I just heard she had Philly on smash until she was killed."

"Ha! Ha! Ha!"

"What's so funny?"

"That was all a myth."

"How do you know?"

"How, because I'm Tanya Montana!"

"Stop playing."

"I'm not."

"What happen?"

"Tha Feds started getting on to me so I faked Tanya's death."

"How?"

"Nobody knew what I look like, so it was easy to do then go on living my life."

"Damn you still holding then."

"I got a little something," she said wit a devious smile.

"Now I'm actually messaging wit tha infamous Tanya Montana."

"Tha one and only."

"Now it's all coming to light."

"What is?"

"How you would tell me certain things that were in tha game."

"I just wanted you to be safe not to mention I love you."

"Don't worry your secret is safe wit me Tanya," I said winking at her."

"Boy you funny."

"I got to make sure my baby's mother is a'ight."

"Always Baby always!"

"Let's go."

"Yeah cause I'm ready to get some real good lovin' tonight."

"You get that all tha time."

"True but I need that special love making tonight if you know what I'm talking about."

"I definitely know what you're talking about."

When Camron came back we asked for tha check.

"Would you like a doggy bag?"

I looked at all tha food that was left on table and said yes. Five minutes later, he was back wit two doggie bags and tha check. I paid tha bill plus left him a $50 tip.

"Damn Big Homie I appreciate tha tip."

"No problem I'm always lookin' to help a brother out anyway I can."

(BEYONCÉ TRACK 6 VOLUME 15)

"Oh I see, you want some head on tha way home."

"Nah I just wanted to hear my shit that's all." She started to unbuckle my pants anyway.

"Last time you did this we almost crashed."

"I know so keep ya eyes on tha road this time."

"How can I when you have a nigga spaced out?"

"Tha same way I keep my composure when you do it to me."

"Babe you hardly keep ya composure."

"I know, listen to me lying it sounded good though."

"Yeah, it sounded real good."

Liz gave me head all tha way home which only took me 15 minutes since I floored it tha whole way there. Not even 10 minutes later after pulling up I was up in Liz like my life depended on it.

"Yes, Yes, Yes Daddy!"

"Who's pussy is this?"

"OH MY GOD IT'S YOURS DADDY IT'S YOURS JUST DON'T STOP! FUCK THIS PUSSY, UMM HMM FUCK THIS PUSSY!" Tha more Liz talked tha more I tried to kill it.

"OOOOH RIGHT THERE! THAT'S MY SPOT DADDY!"

"I know that you're spot."

"OOOOH WELL HITTIN' IT, TEAR THIS PUSSY UP! SHIT, SHIT, SHIT! I'M ABOUT TO CUM!!"

"Let it out then."

Before she could utter another word, Liz was shaking like a stripper at Magic City. Once I knew she was cumin I started to play wit her clit while still stroking her knowing that this would send her into a frenzy like a body in shark infested water.

"YEEEEEES DADDY! SHIIIIT! OOOOHH! HMMM GOD DAMN!!

Wit out saying another word Liz flipped me over and started riding me like a horse in tha Kentucky Derby.

"OH SHIT! I'M ABOUT TO NUT!"

"HOLD ON DADDY LET ME CUM WIT YOU!!!" Five minutes later, we both let out a big moan and collapsed on tha bed.

"Amir you got to stop fucking me like that."

"That was just tha beginning, now it's time for round two."

"Well bring it on then," she said spreading her legs wide open.


Two hours later, we both lay there thinking about tha lovemaking session we just had.

"Amir."

"Yes."

"I love you."

"I love you too. You know Imma pamper you while you pregnant right?"

"So, I can save my money is what you're telling me?"

"Sure is. I still can't get over you being tha infamous Tanya Montana."

"Hey, don't ever judge a book by its cover."

"I don't."

"So, let me ask you again, what made you leave tha game?"

"I have too much to lose plus I don't need tha money; Shit I got too much."

"Baby you can never have too much money."

"I know it just sounds good to say."

"Ha! Ha! Ha!"

# CHAPTER 28

## Tha Births, Truth Revealed, and Consequences

"Push Baby Push!"

"AAAAAAH!!! I am pushing Oh My God! I'm never having sex again AAAAAAH!! Meanwhile two doors down Jazz was going through tha same thing.

"AAAAAAH SHHHIIT!!! I hate you Fourty!"

"Baby just push."

"You try to do this Mr. Bad Ass!"

Roxy was tha only one not going through tha motions you would think it wasn't her first time as calm as she was.


45 minutes later, Mayla pushed out an 8lb. 7oz baby boy who looked just like Tex. Two minutes later, Jazz spit out a beautiful 6lb. baby boy while Roxy had a 7lb. baby girl.

"Oh My God she's beautiful."

"Look who her dad is."

"Boy pleeeease."

"So, you saying I'm not sharp?"

"Baby you know you sharp, but she looks like her mother."

"Oh My God look at her looking like Stylz," Paradise said.

"Don't you say nothing."

"I'm not sayin' Shit."

"What did I miss?"

"Nothing you just confirmed what I already knew."

"Can I hold her?"

"Yeah but be careful wit her."

"Listen to you already."

"This daddy's little diva."

"She is going to be so spoiled."

"Yes she is," Fourty said kissing all over her face, "what did you name her?"

"Samya."

"That's pretty."

"Thank you somebody didn't like it."

"I never said I didn't like it I just preferred Amia."

"I like both of them."

"So, what is it Samya Amia?"

"No, it's Samya Malaysha."

"May I make a suggestion?"

"Sure."

"How about Malaysha Samya?" Fourty started smiling.

"What?"

"I told her It sounded better that way."

"Well then we can change it."

"Baby you can leave it tha way it is if you want to."

"No, I can't lie I do like Malaysha Samya better."

"Well, that's all it is then. Let me go see Jazz and Fourty's son," said Paradise.

"You already seen Lil' Tex."

"Yes, he's a sharp green eye little boy."

"Green eyes?"

"Yup, don't ask me how when his parents both have hazel eyes."

"Ya guess is good as mine." Malaysha was beautiful as well she had a head full of curly hair wit brown eyes.

"I'll be back before I leave."

"A'ight and thanks for tha balloons Paradise."

"Girl you know that ain't about nothing."


When I walked into Jazz's room I couldn't help but smile when I saw her son.

"Oh My God he is so adorable."

"Thank you."

"What's his name?"

"Nah'cee."

"That's cute and different."

"Look at all that hair on his head."

"I know right."

"Bitch I know he don't got no gray eyes?"

"Yes, he does just like his Aunt Classy."

"I'm telling you y'all wit these pretty ass babies."

"Oh, you saw Roxy and Mayla babies?"

"Yup, you know their all about 10 minutes apart?"

"Seriously?"

"Yeah."

"Nah'cee and Lil' Tex will protect Malaysha."

"How do you know her name?"

"Fourty said that's what he wanted to name her if Jazz..."

"You two are Fourty and Jazz? Shit I'm all messed up, you know what I meant."

"Nigga you must be high."

"Nah, just happy that's all."

"I don't blame you."

Two days later, Mayla, Roxy, and Jazz all sat around wit Lil' Tex, Nah'cee, and Malaysha."

"Bitch I'm still trying to figure out where Lil' Tex got those green eyes from."

"His father."

"Tex has hazel eyes."

"Hazel eyes that turn green as well as gray."

"God Damn I never knew that, I'm jealous."

"Of what?"

"Y'all had these pretty ass babies."

"You know what to do about that."

"I'm not that jealous."

"Ha! Ha! Ha! I heard that."

"How does it feel to be a mom?"

"I can't speak for them but I'm loving it so far."

"Well you better enjoy these nights and days all they do is sleep, eat, and shit right now."

"I can't wait til my six weeks."

"UNH, UNH, UNH, that's how you got Lil' Tex."

"Oh well a bitch need some dick in her life."

"Let me find out you dick whipped."

"Shit I might be."

"Bitch ain't no might in it."

"You got a nerve."

"No I don't cause I know I have my man's dick."

"So, Ms. Paradise what's tha deal wit you and Amir?"

"I don't even know I haven't been seeing him to much lately."

"Why?"

"He's been spending time wit his other broads I guess."

"Fourty told me that he's getting out tha game, so he's been making sure his biz-nesses are tight."

"I thought they were legit?"

"They are, he says he just wants to make sure nobody's been on no bullshit."

"So, he really leaving tha game alone huh?"

"Yup, they all are done Tex hasn't hustled since I had tha baby he's been making sure his restaurant is straight."

"What kind of restaurant is he opening a soul seafood joint on South Street."

"As long as tha food is jumping he'll kill them on South Street."

"I think tha grand opening is in two weeks."

"Shit I'll be there."

"Me too."

"We'll all be there."


"Hey what's going on in here?"

"Hey Baby, nothing we just chatting."

"Probably more like gossiping."

"Babe I just came from tha restaurant that Shit is off tha chain I can't wait til tha grand opening."

"So, you finally decided to get out tha game huh?"

"Yeah, I've got all I can get out of it so it's time to go legit."

"Most people won't stop til tha Feds run down on them."

"Nah not me, I have too much to lose," Tex said kissing Mayla and picking up Lil' Tex.

"I know that's right Baby we need you around for tha long haul."

"I plan to be around for tha long haul."

"Baby just in case you need to hear it I love you."

"Mayla I love you too."

"Awe ain't that cute."

"Man go head wit that Roxy."

"What? That's cute, I remember when Mayla was playing hard to get."

"Bitch I wasn't playing hard to get I was trying to see if he wanted me or just some pussy."

"I wanted both."

"You got both and some."

"Sure did," he said kissing on his first born.

"It took me a minute but once I got her she was hooked like a fish."

"Boy pleeeease."

"He ain't lying."

"He sure ain't tha way you was talking our heads off about him. Oh My God y'all he is so nice, he is so compassionate, he's this, he's that."

"Damn, y'all got me blushing now, I never knew you felt like that about me Mayla."

"I didn't think that it was important as long as you know I love you."

"What time do you want to go pick up Lil' Tex crib?"

"I thought they were delivering it."

"Nah, I wanted to make sure it didn't get Fucked up."

"It's up to you they were all about to go anyway."

"Yeah, let me get home wit Malaysha before Stylz starts calling me asking where his daughter is."

"Same thing I go through wit Fourty."

"Y'all have to understand these are their children."

"Shit I constantly call Mayla and ask about my son."

"Yes you do."

"Be quiet, you love when I call to check up on y'all."

"I never said I didn't."

"A'ight Mayla we'll talk to you later on."

"OK."

On my ride home, I couldn't help but to think what it would be like to be pregnant by Amir. As soon as I pulled up to my house my phone started to ring.

"Hello."

"OK I'll be right in."

*Damn it's always something going on at this job.* I decided to run in and make me a bite to eat first.

"Twist why are we hanging out here?"

"I need to see something."

"See what?"

"One of my inside Connects said that someone we trust was sleeping wit tha enemy."

"Hey ain't that Shorty right there?"

"Where?"

"Getting out that Benz."

"Oh, you talking about Roxy's people."

"Yeah."

"I'll be right back."

"What tha Fuck you up to?"

"Just trust me on this."

As soon as I walked in tha building I saw what I needed to see I couldn't believe my eyes or my ears. I slid back out tha some way I slid in.


"What's up? Did you see what you had to see?" I didn't answer I just picked up my phone and then pushed send.

"What up Big Homey?"

"What's up Twist."

"I need you to get ery body together and meet me at tha spot."

"When?"

"Now!"

"A'ight I'll make tha calls."

"Twist you wanna fill me in on what's going on?" He didn't say Shit he just turned his phone around.

"Oh Shit! What tha Fuck is going on?" Twist didn't have to say anything because his face and body language said it all.

"Let me see that again," I asked still not convince, "damn!"

By tha time we pulled up to tha spot Fourty, Tex, Stylz, and Amir were already there.

"What's up y'all?"

"You tell us."

"Yeah, what was so important that you needed to see us right away?"

"We have a problem."

"We aren't in tha game anymore or have you forgot?"

"Nah, I haven't forgotten but this is something that concerns all of us."

"Spit it out, don't keep us in tha dark."

"They say a picture is worth a thousand words, so I'll just show you." When they saw tha image on tha phone all of their mouths flew open.

"Oh Shit!"

"Mafucka!"

"Dirty Mafucka!" Amir didn't say Shit, but I knew something was wrong.

"I'll take care of it for you."

"Nah, Imma handle this one."

"Yo you a'ight?"

"Yeah I'm straight."

*Damn let me call Amir and see if he wants to have dinner later tonight.* After three rings he picked up.

"Hello Amir."

"Hey."

"Are you busy tonight?"

"Actually, I was going to call you and ask if you wanted to have a nice dinner wit me tonight?"

"Yes of course I will."

"A'ight I'll pick you up around 9 o'clock."

"A'ight see you then."


It was A little before 9 o'clock when I arrived to pick up Paradise. I had to admit, she was looking good as Hell wit that pink Elevee dress on.

"Hey Babe, I hope I'm not overdressed."

"Nah you fine, I hope you don't have to work in tha morning."

"I do but I can always call off."

"Yeah, that might be a good idea, we have a long night ahead of us."

"That sounds great."

"You might want to pack an overnight bag."

"OK it won't take me long, but you can come in if you want."

"Yeah I need to use tha bathroom." After I used tha bathroom I started to look around just being nosey.

"Amir I'll be right down."

"Take ya time, I'm not rushing you."

I went to tha dining room and pulled out one of her drawers and found an interesting picture that I placed in my pocket.

"Sorry it took me so long."

"You a'ight, you ready?"

"Yeah I'm ready. Where we going if you don't mind me asking?"

I didn't want to spoil tha surprise, so I said, "It's a surprise."

"Ooooh I like surprises."

"Well you'll love this one then."

Two hours later, we were pulling up in Baltimore.

"Hey wake up sleepyhead."

"Damn how long was I asleep?"

"About an hour."

"Where are we?"

"B-More."

"Baltimore?"

"Yup, good old B-More."

After checking in I made reservations to one of tha finest restaurants B-More had.

"After we eat how would you feel about hitting a club?"

"I'm cool wit it." After eating we headed to Hammer Jacks to get our party on.

"Damn this line is long as Hell. I hope we can pay to get upfront cause ain't no way I'm standing in this long ass line." We parked and then walked to tha front of tha line.

"Tha line starts back there My Man."

"Yeah well I was kind of hoping to get in V.I.P.," I said handing him three crisp one hundred-dollar bills.

He lifted tha red rope to let us though, "Enjoy yourselves."

"Damn it's packed in this piece and hot too."

"Come on let's head to V.I.P. so we can get our drinks."

"Thought you would never..."

"Just come on," I said cutting her off before she could finish.

"Is that how you feel?"

I looked at her and then said, "Imma show you how I feel later."

"Umm that sounds good to my ears."

Once we got to V.I.P. I had tha bar maid bring me two bottles of that Ace of Spade along wit a bottle of Bombay Sapphire.

"Damn you trying to get a bitch drunk."

"Hey that's tha best sex drunk sex."

"You think so?"

"So, I've been told anyway."

"Yeah I bet."

"For real."

After about four bottles of Spade and two bottles of Bombay a bitch was more than ready to get her freak on. I sat on Amir's lap and started grinding on him to tha beat which only causes his penis to become erect.

"Umm I see somebody couldn't hold his excitement."

"What do you say we get out of here?"

"Thought you would never ask."


Twenty minutes later, we were pulling up to tha hotel entrance.

"Would you like me to park your car Sir?"

"Nah I got it."

"Let me out so I can go up and be ready for you."

"That's what's up."

I started to think about all tha ways I can give it to her. After parking I stopped in tha bar to have a few drinks before going upstairs to Paradise.


"Damn I was beginning to think you went back to Philly."

"Ha! Ha! Ha! You got jokes huh?"

"No."

"I stopped at tha bar to have a few drinks."

"Did you bring some up wit you?"

"Yeah, I got a bottle."

"Well pour me a cup please."

"You don't need no more to drink."

"Pleeeease I'm grown, I know what I can do or don't need."

"Do you?"

"Sure do and right about now I need some of that dick of yours."

"Say no more."

Two hours later, Paradise was sound asleep. I decided to run out and get a few things we would need once she woke up.


"What tha Fuck? What's going on?" I asked not able to move my hands.

"I was hoping you could tell me."

"Amir what are you talking about?"

"Paradise let's not play this game or should I just call you Agent Sharp?" Tha look on her face said it all, "you see, I have a lot of friends in high places."

"Amir let me explain."

"Oh please do, tha floor is all yours."

"At first I was trying to do my job, but I started falling in love wit you."

"Bitch please, you don't love me!"

"Yes I do, that's why I compromised my job."

"How tha Fuck did you do that?"

"By giving my superiors false information. Amir I was planning on telling you tha truth today."

"Sure you were."

"I was."

"Does Mayla know you're a Fed?"

"No, she doesn't know anything; she thinks I'm a civil lawyer."

"It all makes sense now, you trying to get me to deal wit ya so called cousin. It was all a set up."

"At that time, it was but you didn't go for it."

"Cause I'm not slow, how do you think I've lasted this long in tha game?" I screwed tha silencer on my pistol and watched her eyes grow.

"Amir you don't have to do this I love you."

"Paradise, I don't believe you nor do I trust you. There's no way I can let you leave here alive."

"Amir have you ever done anything around or in front of me?"

"To think I was going to settle down wit you. Damn I'm a Fuckin' Fool!"

"No, you were just following ya heart."

"You're right, now my heart is telling me to put an end to this."

"Amir let's just cut tha Bullshit, you already have a significant other."

"I do but you were going to be a part of my life as well," I watched as tha tears started to roll down her cheeks, "Paradise it has been good these past two years I can't front. Maybe at another time we would have been tha perfect fit but I'm unfortunately this relationship has definitely run its course."

"Amir I just want you to know that I honestly do love you."

"Yeah I love you too."

A smile crept across Paradise's face and those would be tha last words she heard. (PIT, PIT, PIT, PIT, PIT, PIT, PIT, PIT, CLICK, CLICK, CLICK)

Amir kept squeezing far after tha clip was empty. He looked at her lifeless body and picked up his phone. He waited a few seconds and then said, "It's done."

After hanging up he wiped tha whole room down and quietly left.

# CHAPTER 29

## Tha Conclusion, Now and One Year Later

"Hey Amir."

"Hey Mayla."

"Have you seen or talked to Paradise?"

"No not since last week why?"

"I've been trying to call her, but she isn't picking up."

I wanted to say because she's dead but instead I just said, "I just figured she was working."

Tex looked at me wit a slight smile.

"Baby I'll see you later I'm about to shoot some hoops wit tha fellas."

"A'ight, if I'm not here when you get back I'll be at Roxy's."


When we were outside I asked Tex if he thought that what I had done was justified.

"Of course I do, if you didn't do it I would have."

"Thanks Tex."

"For what?"

"Letting me know that I made tha right choice."

"It was tha right choice, but I know you had feelings for her."

"Yeah I can't front, I had feelings, but I couldn't let that be my downfall. Crazy thing is she didn't have Shit on me because I never talked biz-ness around her or made moves wit her in tha car."

"Did you handle tha other thing before you killed her?"

"You know I did."

"A'ight lets go bust some ass."

- 269 -

> *Dear Chief,*
>
> *I am handing in my resignation, I can't do this. I fell in love wit tha target, so I am resigning and moving away. Please do not try to find me; I'm sorry Chief I never meant for this to go down like this.*
>
> *Yours truly, Paradise Sharp*

Tha Chief stood there speechless taking tha letter and put it back inside tha envelope then placed it into his top desk drawer.

One year later...

Tex, Lil' Tex, and Mayla sat in his restaurant eating a nice meal that Tex had prepared for tha three of them.

"Baby this is a good meal."

"Good," Lil' Tex said wit his mouth full of chicken.

"Tex I love you."

"Do you?"

"Boy stop playing wit me for I hurt you."

"Mayla I really love you too and that's why I was wondering if you would be my wife?" I asked pulling out tha huge rock I had specially made.

"Oh My God! Yes! Yes! Yes! I'll be ya wife," she said holding her hand out, so I can put tha ring on her finger.

Roxy and Stylz were enjoying themselves on their honeymoon. Amila was in tha suite next door wit tha nanny. Stylz and Roxy's wedding was definitely one to remember.

Jazz and Fourty decided to buy a house and move in together so that Nah'cee could grow up in a two-parent home. They also opened up a bakery in West Philly.

As for Amir, him and Liz ended up having twins named Amir and Amirah who were now six-months-old looking just like Amir. Even though he loved Liz he still had Allisa on tha side. All of his biz-nesses were doing extremely well, and he felt good being out of tha game.

Buck and Twist still had tha whole Philly in a chokehold; nothing moved wit out their say so. Sometime things do get complicated...

# ABOUT THE AUTHOR

My name is Jerz Toston, I reside in Wilmington, Delaware. First, thanks to my fans for your continued support. This is my 4th book titled Compromised. My other three books titled Street Dreamz: Ery Thing Ain't What It Seems, Who Can U Trust? and Betrayal & Deceit are available now on all on-line bookstores. Also, you can call my publisher directly at 877.782.5550 x100 and them shipped to ya door.

Writing books is my passion and I'll continue to give you page turners. Just call me ya Fav Authors Fav Author.

Betrayal & Deceit

Who Can U Trust?

Street Dreamz